D0896770

MOUNTAIN RETREAT

A MYSTERY THRILLER NOVELLA

MICHAEL MERSON

Mountain Retreat, Copyright © Michael Merson 2022

All rights reserved.

No part of this publication may be reproduced, stored in a retrieval system, or transmitted, in any form or by any means, electronic, mechanical, photocopying, recording or otherwise, nor translated into a machine language, without the written permission of the publisher.

Condition of sale
This book was sold subject to the condition that it shall not, by way of trade or otherwise, be lent, re-sold, hired out or otherwise circulated in any form of binding or cover other than that in which it was published and without a similar condition including this condition being imposed on the subsequent purchaser.

The moral right of the author had been asserted.

This was a work of fiction. Any resemblance to actual persons, living or dead, events and organizations was purely coincidental.

ISBN: 978-1-956412-22-2 (eBook)
ISBN: 978-1-956412-23-9 (Trade Paperback)

Edited by Novel Nurse Editing

Cover Design by: G•S Cover Design Studio
https://www.gsstockphotography.com/

MOUNTAIN RETREAT

PROLOGUE
DENVER

The airport was crowded with travelers flying in and out of Denver. Porter Rollins and his partner Lance Lawson stood around the baggage area, watching for the woman to arrive. The men weren't her friends or family. As a matter of fact, they had never met her, and they indeed weren't there to greet her with open arms. Still, they were there to make sure she was taken care of and soon. Porter was a retired US Navy SEAL, and Lance was a dishonorably discharged US Army Ranger. The two were hired hitmen, bodyguards, and anything else that required a man with a gun whose moral compass was anything but true. For the last year, the men had been working for Senator Vince Livingston as bodyguards and fixers. Senator Livingston was a powerful man in the world of politics. The senator, like many corrupt politicians, got to where he was with the help of bribes and other illegal contributions. He also benefited from his wife, Linsey, and her inheritance.

All the two hired men knew about the woman was that she was supposed to arrive at five o'clock from Jacksonville, Florida, and the senator wanted her dead. The senator had provided them with a few photos of the target and instructions on what he expected to happen. Porter had also been ordered to hire someone else to do the job but to make sure it was done. Three days ago, Porter hired an old Navy buddy who was in desperate need of money.

Lance first spotted the woman when she walked into the luggage area. He inconspicuously kept an eye on her as she made her way to the baggage carousel and waited for her bags. He took out his cell phone and called Porter.

"Carousel number four, blonde, with her hair in a ponytail, black yoga pants, and white T-shirt," he explained.

"I got her. Get the car and meet me outside in the arrival pickup area," Porter instructed and ended the call. He then stood closer to the woman and looked her over. He figured she was five feet five and probably weighed a hundred and fifteen pounds. She was athletic and beautiful. *What a waste,* he thought.

After the woman grabbed her large backcountry backpack, she walked outside to the airport's rideshare area. She looked for the SUV she was expecting. When a black Ford Explorer pulled up, she opened the back door, tossed her backpack inside, and sat down. Porter quickly walked by and placed a magnetic, electronic tracker on the trunk as he passed. He then watched the Explorer pull out from under the garage, right as Lance pulled up.

Porter opened the passenger door and sat. "Go!" he ordered. He took his cell phone out and started tracking the device.

After three miles on the interstate, Lance caught up with the woman. "Where's our guy?"

"He's near I-Seventy and Highway Seventy-Four. He's going to do it somewhere in the town of Evergreen. Mr. Livingston told me that's where she's meeting some other people," Porter answered.

"Are you sure we can trust this old friend of yours?" Lance asked.

"We'll see. He's the only one I could find who could take the job."

Lance shook his head. "I don't like using outside help. We should've done this ourselves."

"Livingston doesn't want this to blow back on him. He thinks you and I could be blowback. I didn't agree with him, but he's the boss," Porter explained.

Lance changed lanes and looked over at his partner. "This kind of job should have cost a lot more."

Porter kept his eyes on the phone. "Yeah, but we both know Livingston is a cheap bastard."

After nearly an hour on the road, Lance pointed. "Look, we're getting close. Call your guy," he said, seeing Evergreen's exit sign.

Porter scrolled through his contacts, found his guy's number, and called it.

"It's me. She's in a black Ford Explorer that's on the offramp now," Porter said when the hired killer answered.

Jeff Doyle sat in an old moving truck that he had recently stolen from a storage unit. Jeff had once been a police officer with the Denver Police Department. He'd been forced to resign over accusations of misconduct during traffic stops. The allegations came from multiple women who alleged Officer Doyle sexually harassed them. Some of the women also alleged that Doyle showed up at their homes, places of employment, and followed them when they were out at night on the weekends. The news media got the story and ran with it. Officer Doyle resigned when the Internal Affairs Division asked that he come in for an interview with his attorney. No charges were ever officially filed. Jeff heard the city had paid his accusers an undisclosed amount to settle their cases. Now, the disgraced police officer worked for whoever called Doyle Investigations.

Jeff received his private investigator's license soon after leaving the department. He moved out of Denver and settled in a small mountain community twenty miles west of Colorado Springs. Most days, Jeff checked on the security systems in expensive vacation cabins for wealthy homeowners who spent their weekends and holidays in the mountains. On other days, Jeff tracked down and photographed cheating spouses. He also worked as a bouncer at bars and strip clubs. Sometimes, like today, he did a little wet work that paid much better than the other jobs he took.

Jeff hung up the phone and waited until he saw the black Explorer turn onto Highway Seventy-Four. When the SUV passed, he pulled in behind it. The highway was busy with commuters rushing home to start their weekend early. The parking lot of the shopping center was crowded with customers. It was a lousy location to do what Jeff had been hired to do, but that was where the Explorer had turned into.

"Damn it!" Jeff mumbled. He looked around. The contract killer needed to act quickly and privately. He watched the Explorer drive through the parking lot. Then, to the hired gunman's surprise, the driver pulled the SUV up and parked on the side of the large building. They were out of sight of any witnesses. Now was the moment. Jeff pulled up behind the Explorer, quickly walked to the passenger side of the SUV, and fired one shot from his 9mm at the driver and another at the rear seat passenger. The silencer muffled the gunshots, but Jeff still had to act fast. He rushed back to the moving truck, opened the back, and pulled out the tire ramps.

Porter and Lance watched the entire event from the other side of the highway.

"What's he doing now?" Lance asked.

Porter shook his head from side to side. "I don't know."

The hired killer rushed back to the Explorer, opened the driver's door, and pushed the driver's lifeless body into the passenger seat. He then drove the SUV into the back of the moving van.

Lance looked around. "No! He was supposed to leave her there to be found. The senator said that she's got to be found!"

"I know," Porter replied as he tried calling Jeff, who wasn't answering.

Jeff felt his cell phone vibrating in his pocket, but he was too busy to answer it. After securing the SUV in place, he jumped out of the truck, closed the door, and looked around before getting back into the cab. He then drove out of the area. The killer knew he was supposed to leave the woman there but after some thought, he felt it was better for her to be found someplace where there were fewer witnesses.

"Follow him!" Porter shouted as he continued to try to call the hired gunman.

Lance nodded and spun the car around without making sure the road was clear. Both men were surprised when a passenger van slammed into their car's left front quarter panel, sending them into the guardrail. Lance was knocked unconscious, but Porter still had his wits about him. He jumped out and found the moving van heading out of the area.

"Damn it!" he yelled and ran back to Lance.

The arrival of a late spring storm brought cooler temperatures and a blanket of heavy wet snow covering the Colorado Mountains. A cabin sat a quarter mile off the main fire service road, just outside the popular fishing area of Deckers. The mountain home was built to appear rugged, but upon closer inspection, it was anything but. Large logs that were lightly stained sat upon a three-foot wall of beautifully colored river rock. The cabin's red roof was made of metal that provided a gentle, rhythmic pattering during summer rainstorms. Jeff sat inside the luxury mountain cabin in a leather chair in the living room, enjoying his freshly poured Godfather. He peacefully watched the falling snow accumulate on the deck outside. The bourbon and its slight touch of amaretto were a perfect combination to go along with the Fuente Fuente Opus X that he smoked. The cigar was from the Dominican Republic, and it was expensive, but Jeff believed it was requisite on nights like this.

The hired killer placed his empty glass on the table. He sat back, closed his eyes, and listened to the soothing sounds of "The

Irish Blessing" as it softly played throughout the cabin's many speakers.

"Please, help me!" The woman's voice echoed from the basement, interrupting the melody.

Jeff opened his eyes, sat up, and peered at the knotty alder door under the stairs. He waited for her to quiet herself but then heard her again.

"Please, help me!"

Jeff's eyes narrowed, and his forehead furrowed as he reached for the remote control lying on the table next to the empty bottle of bourbon. He picked up the small device and increased the volume, hoping to drown out the woman's cries. Once again, he leaned back and closed his eyes, but only for a brief moment.

The sound of metal on metal clanking and the woman's desperate pleas for help disturbed him again. Jeff clenched his fist, lifted himself out of the chair, turned the music off, and staggered toward the door to the basement. He angrily reached for the knob with his right hand but missed it completely, causing him to fall forward against the door. With his head resting on the wood, he whispered, "Bitch! I should have just killed her earlier when I realized she was still alive." Jeff was drunk, and he knew it. Thoughts of the day haunted him in his semiconscious state.

After the shooting, he'd stopped to dump the Explorer in a deep ravine near the town of Conifer, and that was when Jeff discovered that the woman in the back seat was still alive. Apparently, his bullet had merely grazed her head, knocking her unconscious temporarily. When Jeff saw her, he couldn't resist, and his thoughts turned darker as he watched her struggling to regain consciousness. He thought she was beautiful, and he wanted her. For a little while anyway, and she wasn't going to be his first.

Jeff had used the butt of his pistol to knock her out once more. He removed her from the Explorer and sent it and the driver into the ravine. Jeff found the woman's cell phone and saw she had missed a few text messages from the people she had apparently planned on meeting. Jeff responded to those texts, pretending to be her. He apologized to her friends, informing them that she'd had an emergency and wouldn't make it this weekend. He then tossed her cell phone into the ravine. Finally, he secured the woman and brought her back to the cabin. He handcuffed her to a metal gas pipeline in the basement. Jeff had his way with her while she drifted in and out of consciousness. He had planned on spending more time with her over the weekend, but now he decided that was a bad idea.

"To hell with it!" he shouted before opening the door and heading into the basement with his hunting knife in hand.

The woman was confused. She was naked and tied to a metal pipe, which she was loudly banging on with a wrench she had found under the boiler.

Jeff stood over her. "Why can't you just be quiet?" he shouted.

"Please help me," she cried.

Jeff clenched his fist, reached back with the knife, and brought the butt of it down onto his victim's head. The woman slumped forward, so he reached down and began to unhandcuff her. The drunken man fumbled with the key and cuffs for a few minutes before he could open the shackles. Jeff reached for the woman's wrist and was surprised to discover that she was not unconscious. He dropped the handcuffs to the concrete.

His victim swung the wrench into the side of his head. Jeff fell backward. He was dazed, and as he crawled around trying to collect himself, the woman ran by him on her way out of the basement.

"No!" he yelled as he staggered to the stairway. Jeff got to his feet, steadied himself against the wall, and tried to clear his hazy vision.

The woman ran up the stairs and burst onto the cabin's main floor. She stopped and looked around. On the back of a couch, she saw a blanket. She grabbed it and wrapped herself up. She didn't know what was happening, but she knew she was in danger. Suddenly, she heard the man coming up the stairs. The hostage panicked. She ran for what looked like the front door and opened it.

Jeff got to the basement door and found her standing in the entryway. "No, come back here!"

Run. Just run! she thought as she looked between the falling snow outside and her kidnapper. Without another thought, she sprinted out the door into the dark forest surrounding the cabin. She heard him running after her, but she kept running barefoot through the wet snow, passing one large conifer tree after another. She didn't know where she was or where she was desperately running to, but it didn't matter. The man she had escaped from was dangerous, and anything was better than allowing him to recapture her. She was out of breath, bleeding from her head, and things were blurry. She stopped running when she found herself at the edge of a cliff. There was no place for her to run.

Jeff crested a small hill where he found the woman standing a few dozen yards away. He smiled, raised his pistol, and took aim.

The woman turned just as the bullet ripped through her arm. She fell backward off the cliff and slid down the snow-covered hillside and into the frigid waters of the South Platte River.

The killer rushed over to stare down the side of the mountain but couldn't see anything. *She's gotta be dead,* he thought. After a few minutes of watching down into the darkness, Jeff glanced at his watch. "Nearly four," he said, before turning and starting back to the cabin.

The sun was rising when Brody Katz pulled his rebuilt customized 1989 Land Rover Defender off the main road and into the parking area near the bridge. The forty-one-year-old outdoorsman was looking forward to his day of fly fishing on the South Platte River. Brody wanted to challenge his angler skills, so he selected an area of water with deep pockets, riffles, and slow runs. He looked around at the fresh spring snow that had fallen the night before and took a moment to admire its beauty. As the off-duty deputy stepped from the bank, he looked down into the crystal-clear water and saw a rainbow trout swimming above the gravel bed. Brody smiled. *It's going to be a good day,* he thought.

Brody walked out to the center of the river toward what looked like a deep pocket on the opposite side. The experienced angler brought his pole up, his line back, and was ready to cast when he spotted something on the riverbank's edge. He dropped his rod to his side and crept toward what he thought was a colorful blanket someone had discarded in the river. When he got closer, he reached down and grabbed a corner of it. He pulled the blanket backward, revealing the naked body of a woman. Brody released the blanket, stumbled back, and fell into the water.

Brody quickly picked himself up out of the river and stared at the body for a moment. *Relax! You've seen a dead body before,* he told himself and started toward her. She was on her stomach. Most of her body was on the bank; only her legs were in the water. "What happened to you?" Brody asked as he reached down to pull her farther onto the bank.

"Help me," the woman whispered. It startled the fisherman.

Brody dropped the woman's arm, and once again, he fell back into the river. "She's alive!" he shouted. He lifted himself out of the water, rushed over to pick her up, and started back across the river. Brody fell twice with her in his arms, but he picked her back up with ease. When he got to his Defender, he sat her in the passenger seat and turned the vehicle on. The deputy wasted no time and headed toward the mountain town of Woodland Park, where the closest hospital was located. After ten minutes, he got cell phone service, called nine one one, and informed the dispatcher that he was speeding to the hospital with a medical emergency.

Brody made it to the emergency room in about twenty minutes. He was met by the Teller County Sheriff and two other deputies.

"Brody, what happened?" Sheriff Paul Kendrick asked.

"Help me!" Brody called as he opened the passenger door, revealing the woman he had found.

The sheriff's eyes widened, and he rushed over with his deputies. They pulled the woman out and laid her on the gurney the hospital staff had wheeled over.

Brody, the sheriff, and the other deputies watched as medical staff treated the unknown woman in the emergency room.

Doctor Alder examined his patient and found the wound on the patient's shoulder. "This is a gunshot wound!"

Sheriff Kendrick turned toward Brody. "Who is she?"

Brody shrugged his shoulders. "I… I don't know. I just found her in the river."

Chapter 1
Alive

After the crash in Evergreen, Lance was airlifted to St. Luke's Medical Center in Denver. He was treated for a severe concussion, minor injuries, and admitted for observation. One of the responding police officers had driven Porter to the hospital. Porter was treated for a bone contusion to his right elbow. After getting discharged, Porter waited in Lance's room for him to awaken. While he waited, he tried to contact Jeff Doyle numerous times. The hired killer seemed to be avoiding Porter, and that bothered him. It didn't make sense for the gunman to not be answering his calls—mainly since Jeff was owed the other half of the money for killing the woman.

Lance came around at about nine, and he and Porter got their stories straight for the police before Porter left the hospital. When he got home, the tired and beaten fixer went to bed with thoughts of Jeff Doyle and the woman. He needed to know where her body was, and that was what he was thinking about when he finally fell asleep sometime after one in the morning.

At seven-thirty, Porter's alarm clock buzzed. He shut it off and looked up at the ceiling. Once again, Porter was questioning Jeff's behavior after shooting the target when he heard his cell phone vibrating on the nightstand beside him. He unplugged it and looked at the caller ID.

He shook his head and answered the call. "Senator Livingston, good morning."

"What happened?" the senator asked in an irate tone.

"We had a small problem, but it should be okay. Lance is in the hospital and—"

"I don't give a damn about Lance! Did you make sure that the job was done?"

Porter hesitated before answering. "Yeah, we watched the guy do it and—"

"So it's just a coincidence that a mystery woman was found in the South Platte River early this morning?"

Porter sat up in bed. "What?"

"Yeah, a *very much alive* woman was found floating in the South Platte near a small mountain community called Deckers," the senator explained.

Porter grabbed the remote off the nightstand and turned on his TV. "Have they identified her?" he asked as images of the river and a hospital were displayed on the screen.

"No, she has not been identified. That's why I called. Should I be worried?"

Porter knew the area where the woman was found, and he also knew it was close to where Jeff Doyle resided. "I don't know yet."

"What do you mean you don't know yet? Either she's her or she's not!" Senator Livingston was in his home, looking out his kitchen window, waiting for his fixer to answer him. His future was at stake. He needed to ensure that the woman was dead and that her body was found.

Porter ran his left hand through his hair. "I don't know, but we should take some precautions just in case."

The senator gripped the sink's edge. "What kind of precautions?" That hadn't been the answer he'd wanted.

"Precautions that will cost money. I'm going to need about

three hundred," Porter reluctantly answered.

The senator's forehead furrowed. He took the phone away from his ear and thought about it. After some deliberation, he put the phone back to his ear. "Do it! And if it hasn't already been done, you do it this time!" the senator ordered.

"I will."

"Also, if your guy messed this up, you take care of him too," the senator ordered and ended the call.

Jeff Doyle had spent the day's early morning hours slowly driving his pickup along Highway 67, searching the river for his victim's body. After two hours, Jeff saw the first news van turning into the parking lot of a convenience store. Twenty minutes later, two more arrived.

He parked near one of the news vans, then walked inside the store, where a reporter was questioning the clerk about the woman found in the river earlier that morning. Jeff quickly turned and had started to walk out when someone tapped him on the shoulder. The hired gunman stopped, slowly turned, and found Amanda Crosse with Channel Ten standing behind him.

"Sir, are you a local, or are you here visiting?" she asked.

Jeff nodded. "I'm local. I just came in to see what all these news vans were doing here."

"A woman was found in the river this morning. The authorities suspect foul play," Amanda explained.

Jeff widened his eyes, hoping to seem surprised. "Really, is she okay?"

"She's in the hospital in Woodland Park. They're not saying much about her condition yet. Hopefully she'll be okay. How would you like to do an interview with me?"

"I'm not that kind of person. I don't want to be on camera," Jeff answered, before turning around and walking out of the store.

When he got back into his truck, he felt his phone vibrating against his leg. He took his phone out and looked at the caller ID. "Damn it!" he mumbled. It was his employer, Porter Rollins. He had ignored his calls the previous day because he'd wanted to have fun with the woman. Now Jeff was avoiding Porter because he needed to fix the problem—before he was a problem… a problem that would need fixing.

Porter spent the rest of his morning trying to connect with Jeff and a friend in the FBI who could keep the woman's identity a secret. He left multiple messages, and at four o'clock in the afternoon, his friend in the FBI called back and agreed to help for a price. Keeping the woman's identity secret cost the senator one hundred and fifty thousand dollars. Porter believed the price was well worth it.

At five thirty, Porter picked Lance up from the hospital, and by seven, they were at the residence of Frank Walters. The two security specialists had a few problems in a small mountain town to take care of, but first they needed to be at the party at Frank's place to make sure no other problems occurred.

Frank Walter's multimillion-dollar mansion was in a gated community in Greenwood Village. The home was fifteen thousand square feet, had twelve bedrooms and fifteen bathrooms, and was protected by a large fence. It was perfect for hosting private parties for people who didn't want to be seen with certain people in public—people like Senator Vince Livingston.

By eight o'clock, the champagne was overflowing, and women were making sure the guests enjoyed their evening. The party's prominent guests were ten men who were either connected, wealthy, or valuable in some way to Senator Vince Livingston. Frank needed the senator in his pocket, and these types of parties helped keep him there. Frank was in the import business, and business was good unless there was an interruption along the delivery route. The senator made sure there were no interruptions by providing Frank with the locations of the state patrol's highway drug interdiction teams.

At midnight, Frank watched the senator walk into one of the second-floor bedrooms with Holly, a high-priced escort who would be keeping the senator busy until morning. All the guests had contributed to the senator's campaign as planned. They were all enjoying the rest of the party similarly to Senator Vince Livingston.

Porter and Lance walked around the party, ensuring no one was taking pictures or spying on the senator. Frank saw Porter near the stairway and decided it was a good time to speak with him.

Frank stood in front of the bodyguard and took a sip of his whiskey before speaking. "What are you doing about the problem in the mountains?"

Porter was caught off guard by the question but was not surprised. He knew the senator had told Frank everything. "We're going out there tomorrow afternoon to take care of it," Porter answered.

Frank laughed. "Who? You and the man over there who can barely walk?"

Porter glanced at Lance, who appeared unsteady on his feet. "He'll be fine."

"No, I'll take care of it. You and your friend keep the senator under control here. He will need a lot of looking after when it finally happens."

Porter pursed his lips together. He knew that the drug dealer was right. "All right, what do you need from me?"

"Just the location of the man who screwed up."

"Okay, what else?"

Frank took another sip and leaned against the handrail. "We need to make sure they can't identify the woman before we can take care of her."

"I already took care of that," Porter replied.

"Good. I'll take care of the rest," Frank said to assure him and walked away.

Porter watched the man as he strolled across the room toward his office. He never liked the five-foot-nine drug dealer with the seven-foot ego, but his opinion didn't matter. Besides, Porter felt better that Frank would be taking care of Jeff Doyle and not him. Porter never enjoyed killing old friends, and now he wouldn't have to.

Deputy Brody Katz sat in the emergency room all day and then later in the hallway outside the recovery room all night. The mystery woman had had minor surgery for the gunshot wound to her shoulder and head, and she was now resting in the recovery room. After bringing the woman to the hospital, Brody had been interviewed by his friend, Detective John Wilson. The off-duty deputy told the detective everything he knew about how and where he had found her.

Brody was a Teller County Deputy, and he had found the woman in Douglas County's jurisdiction. After a lengthy discussion between the Teller County Sheriff and the Douglas County Sheriff it was decided that the Teller County Sheriff's Office would handle the investigation.

Deputy Katz had been on his first day of vacation when he'd found the woman, but he was asked by Sheriff Kendrick to not leave town until they figured out who she was. The sheriff also wanted to ensure that one of his best deputies—and a possible witness to attempted murder—wasn't in danger. Kendrick took Brody off vacation and placed him on temporary administrative leave with pay. Brody had been eliminated as a suspect because he had spent the night before he found the woman at another deputy's home in Deckers. He hoped to get up early and beat the other anglers to the best spots on the river. The other deputy and his family confirmed that Brody arrived early the previous day and that he never left their house until he set out for the river just before dawn.

The hospital's top administrator was busy all day and part of the night, answering questions from the surrounding news stations. The hospital's security officers were just as busy, stopping reporters who tried to sneak into the hospital to get a photo of the mystery woman dubbed the South Platte Floater. Two deputies had been assigned to guard the woman. They positioned themselves at both the entrances of the third floor. Deputy Katz took up residency on the bench outside of the recovery room.

Sheriff Kendrick had given two press conferences, and he'd avoided revealing that one of his off-duty deputies had been the fisherman who'd found the woman. By six o'clock the next morning, everyone in Colorado was once again waking up to the latest news report concerning the South Platte Floater.

A man was tied to the four corners of the bed. He had been tortured by three men, whom he'd once considered friends. Manuel, Jorge, and Pablo were sicarios who worked for the Morales Cartel in the United States. Their main job was to protect the cartel's interest no matter the cost, and tonight they were doing just that. The man they were torturing was a lieutenant in the Morales Cartel who was believed to be stealing. It wasn't until they'd threatened to kill his wife and kids that he finally admitted to it. Now, his wife and children were dead. The sicarios were making an example of him for others who thought about stealing from Mateo Morales.

"Please, I'm sorry. I'll pay it back," the lieutenant pleaded.

Manuel was about to remove the man's fingers with a surgical bone cutter when his cell phone rang. He placed the cutter down, removed his rubber gloves, pulled his cell phone from his pocket, and answered the call. "Bueno," he said.

"It's me. I have a job for you, and it needs to be done in the next couple of days," Frank Walters stated from the comfort of his home office.

Manuel motioned for the other two sicarios to continue beating the lieutenant with baseball bats. At the same time, he stepped into another room to speak with Frank. After a few minutes of listening to the millionaire, Manuel said, "Sí, one or two days," and he abruptly ended the call. He then walked back into the other room.

Manuel looked at the other two men, and in Spanish, he said, "Let's hurry. We have to drive to Colorado." He used his right index finger to give the other two men the throat-cutting signal.

Jorge pulled the man's head back, and Pablo cut his throat. They removed their face shields, paper coveralls, booties, and gloves when they were finished. Before leaving and setting the house on fire, they took pictures of the dead lieutenant and his family and sent them to Mateo Morales.

When they got into the car, Jorge turned and looked at Manuel. "Where are we going in Colorado?" he asked in Spanish.

Manuel entered the address in the Dodge Durango's navigation system and pointed at the screen. "There. Woodland Park," he answered.

Nurse Harper arrived on duty at seven o'clock. She and Nurse Cindy, the night shift nurse, talked about the patients on the floor, their medications, vitals, and things that still needed to be done. They also spoke about the handsome six-foot-one, dark-haired, blue-eyed deputy sleeping on the metal bench outside the mystery woman's room.

"How long has he been here?" Harper asked.

"Since yesterday. He's the one who found her."

"Why did he stay? He doesn't know her. I mean, no one knows who she is yet," Harper said.

Cindy shrugged her shoulders. "I don't know, but he's the male form of Sleeping Beauty. I wouldn't mind waking him with a kiss."

Harper rolled her eyes. "You're so bad!"

Cindy huffed. "Tell me you're not thinking the same thing. Look at him! He hasn't showered, his clothes are a mess, and he's still fine as hell!"

"Go on. Get out of here. I got work to do," Harper said and started down the hall toward Sleeping Beauty.

Harper looked down at the deputy. She then glanced back down the hall to make sure Cindy had left. The nurse bent over and stared at him when she thought the coast was clear. *He is handsome,* she thought. Harper took a deep breath. "Hey, you can't sleep out here all day," she said as she placed her hand on his shoulder and gently shook him.

Brody opened his eyes. It took him a moment to remember where he was and the woman he had found. He sat up, rubbed the sleep from his eyes, and smiled at the nurse. "Hi, I'm Brody."

Harper smiled back. "Hello, Brody. I'm Nurse Harper, and unfortunately, you can't stay here."

"I was just waiting for the um…"

"I know. She's still unconscious, and from what I've seen in her chart, it could be a while before she wakes up," Harper stated in her professional tone.

Brody's smile turned downward. He nodded and reluctantly started to walk away.

Harper saw the expression on his face. *You're such a sucker,* she thought. "How'd you find her?" she asked.

Brody's eyes lit up. "Fishing," he proudly answered.

"Fishing?"

"Yeah," he replied. Brody sat back on the bench, and for about thirty minutes, he told the nurse everything he knew about the mystery woman.

"Wow! What do you think happened to her?" Harper asked.

"I don't know, but the way I found her, it had to be nightmarish. I can't believe she's alive."

Harper read through the woman's chart. "Neither can I. It looks like she was shot in the arm and head. She's been beaten, sexually assaulted, and suffered severe hypothermia."

"She was sexually assaulted?" Brody asked. The deputy knew everything the victim had been through except for the sexual assault.

"You didn't know?" Harper questioned.

Brody looked down. "No. I didn't know."

"Oh my gosh! I shouldn't have said anything. I just—"

Brody held his hands in the air. "It's okay. I would have found it in the report later anyway."

"Please don't tell anyone that I told you," Harper pleaded.

"I won't. Don't worry. The most important thing right now is that we need to find out who she is, contact her family, and let them know she's here."

Harper nodded in agreement and stood. "Yep, I agree. Are you guys sending someone over to get her fingerprints?"

"Yeah, I think Sheriff Kendrick has Detective Wilson coming back at nine to collect them," he answered.

"Good, I'll be here, and when she wakes up… I'll call…" The nurse then remembered they had no one to call other than the sheriff's office.

"Yeah, the sheriff's office," Deputy Katz said.

"The sheriff's office. I'll do that."

Brody turned and started to leave, but an alarm sounded off. Harper turned back toward the nurses' station, where a CNA monitored the floor's patients.

"Room three oh six!" the CNA shouted.

Harper turned to her right and looked at the room number she and Brody were standing in front of. Suddenly the door opened, and the mystery woman groggily stepped out into the hallway.

"Help!" she whispered and collapsed.

Brody caught the patient before she hit the floor. Once again, he had saved the South Platte Floater.

Chapter 2
No Visitors

The Pikes Peak Regional Hospital's parking lot had more than a few news vans sitting in it. Jeff had waited until morning before driving into Woodland Park from his place a few miles out of town. He was hoping to get inside the hospital to finish the job he had been hired to do. During the night, the contract killer realized that the woman may have gotten a good look at him. The way Jeff saw it, he was on the line for kidnapping, rape, and murder. He also had to make things right with Porter.

Getting through the hospital's front entrance was no problem, but getting to the third floor was something completely different. Hospital security guards stood sentry near the elevators and emergency room entrance, checking hospital and visitor badges. Jeff stood there for a moment, thinking about his options. He then pulled the ballcap he found in his truck down lower over his face to conceal it from the surveillance cameras. Next, he put his hands behind his back, and with his left hand, he gripped the thumb of his right. Jeff counted to three in his head, relaxed his right hand, and jerked the thumb. The killer slightly grimaced when he felt the thumb come out of place. Dislocating his thumb when he needed to was a trick Jeff had developed after injuring his hand, sliding headfirst into third base ten years ago. The injury had torn the tendons and ligaments at the joint of his thumb, which provided him with a party trick of sorts. Jeff could escape handcuffs, ropes, and zip ties—all of which earned him free drinks at parties and bars. Now, he would use the trick to fake an injury, which he hoped would gain him access to the hospital.

As he neared the security guard at the emergency entrance, he cradled his right hand in his left. "Is this where I enter to be seen?"

The security officer looked the injured man up and down. "Yeah, do you have an ID?"

"Yeah, I think I can grab it," Jeff answered as he slowly reached back and pulled his wallet out. He removed someone else's driver's license from it.

The security officer merely glanced at the Colorado driver's license. If he had looked more closely, he would have noticed that the man in the photo simply resembled the man standing in front of him. "You can go on back."

"Thanks," Jeff replied. He placed the ID back in his wallet, walked past the guard, and through the double doors into the emergency room's lobby.

"Can I help you?" the receptionist asked when she saw the man walk into the waiting area.

Jeff walked toward the woman and held up his hand. "Yeah, I dislocated my thumb pulling lumber out of my truck."

"Have a seat, and we'll get you checked in."

Jeff looked around. "Can I use the bathroom first?" he asked while pointing toward the men's bathroom.

"Yeah, go right ahead."

Jeff nodded and walked toward the bathroom, which was next to another door that led out of the lobby. When he got to the door, he paused and surveyed the room, and he saw the receptionist get up and walk over to assist a coworker. Suddenly, the door opened, and a phlebotomist walked through it. Jeff took the opportunity and caught the door before it closed. He stepped through it without being seen and started down the hall.

✦

Brody helped Nurse Harper get the woman back into bed.

"Please let me go," the patient kept saying.

Harper rushed into the bathroom and held a washcloth under some cold water. She then returned to the patient and ran the cool cloth against her forehead. "You're safe now. No one will hurt you." Harper reassured her in a low, calm tone.

The woman looked into the nurse's eyes, then reached up and pulled her close. "He hurt me," she cried out and began to sob.

"I know, but you're okay now," Harper whispered while she caringly rubbed her back.

Brody stood there, not knowing what to do or say. He felt deep sadness for the woman.

When the CNA from the nurses' station and Doctor Dawson walked in, Brody stepped back and gave them room to work.

When Doctor Dawson got close to the bed, the patient tried to get up once more and started screaming. He and the CNA held the woman down. "Diazepam!" the doctor ordered another nurse who had entered the room.

The nurse turned and hurried down the hall to retrieve the sedative. The woman grabbed Harper tightly and kicked her legs madly until the other nurse returned. Doctor Dawson rubbed the patient's arm with an alcohol pad and injected the medication.

The mystery woman slowly released Harper, who gently laid her back down.

"Let's get her IV back in place and restrain her to the bed," Doctor Dawson ordered.

Harper gave the doctor a somber expression. "Doctor, do you think that's best? I mean, she was restrained by whoever did this to her," she explained while she held the patient's bruised wrist up for the man to see.

Doctor Dawson's lips turned downward. He knew what he was ordering and knew the patient had been restrained before. "Harper, I know, but she will do more harm to herself if she gets up again. We don't have anyone available to sit with her."

Brody stepped forward to volunteer. "I'll sit with her."

Doctor Dawson shook his head. "I don't know. You're not a nurse or even a CNA—"

"I'm a deputy, and the sheriff ordered that she be guarded. I can do that from right here. I don't think it's a good idea to restrain her. If she tries to get up, I'll call for a nurse," Brody offered.

The doctor looked at the deputy and then at the faces of the three other medical professionals in the room, all of whom were women. He turned toward Brody. "All right, deputy, you can stay here, but if she wakes up or tries to get up, you need to call one of them," Doctor Dawson advised while pointing toward the nursing staff.

"Absolutely," Brody said quickly.

The doctor nodded and walked out. He knew when he was outnumbered. The nurse who had brought the diazepam in for the doctor stepped over to Brody, patted his arm, smiled, and left the room.

The CNA started to walk out of the room, but when she passed the deputy, she stopped, looked him in the eye, smiled, and winked. "I'll have the cafeteria bring up an extra breakfast tray."

Brody nodded and turned toward Harper, who was standing next to the patient's bed, shaking her head.

"What?" Brody asked.

Harper moved toward the deputy and stood in front of him. "Nothing. When she wakes up, give me a call."

Jeff Doyle used the stairwell to access the second floor, where he found the lights dimly lit. The killer soon discovered that the second floor was the coronary care and cardiothoracic unit. Surprisingly, he was able to walk onto the floor and up to the nurses' station without being noticed. On the back of one of the chairs inside the station, he found a nurse's lab coat and an ID badge attached to it. He also found a surgical face mask and hair cover as well. Jeff wasted no time. He grabbed the coat and stepped into the bathroom, where he removed his hat and replaced it with the hair cover and then put on the lab coat. Before exiting the bathroom, he covered his face with the surgical mask and quickly hurried back toward the stairwell. He walked through the door just as two nurses walked out of a patient's room.

Jeff flipped the ID badge backward, put his thumb back in place, and made his way up the stairs to the third floor. When he got to the stairwell door, he cautiously peeked through the square window to look for anyone on the other side before opening it.

Stepping into the hallway, Jeff saw an empty chair sitting next to the stairwell door. He then noticed a deputy sleeping in a chair next to the elevator doors at the other end. He reached to the small of his back and gripped the handle of his pistol. Slowly and quietly, he made his way toward the sleeping deputy.

Suddenly, Jeff heard the door behind him open.

"Good morning."

Jeff spun around and found a second deputy coming out of the bathroom. The lawman had his hand resting on the butt of his duty weapon.

The killer greeted him with a friendly tone. "Good morning."

"Are you part of the day shift?" the deputy asked.

Jeff nodded. "Yeah, I'm just about to come on shift. I work in the lab."

"They make you wear a mask?"

"Yeah, I had a cold and hospital policy requires it. It sucks!"

The deputy nodded. "Yeah, during COVID we had to wear them when we made contact with someone."

"We still do with certain patients." Jeff hoped the deputy continued to buy his lies.

"Yeah, I understand," he said and then looked over his shoulder. "Crazy thing with the woman Deputy Katz found in the river, isn't it?" he said while pointing his thumb over his shoulder toward the mystery woman's room.

"Yeah, it is. I heard you guys were up here guarding her," Jeff replied to the deputy, who he believed was the type of person who overshared.

The deputy took a deep breath and blew it out, puffing his cheeks. "I can't believe she made it. The doctors say someone shot her in the head, beat her, raped her, and then shot her in the arm."

"The arm?" Jeff asked, bewildered.

The lawman lifted his arm and pointed to the outside of it. "Yeah, it looks like the bullet just passed through the outside flesh. I guess the pervert was a bad shot!"

Jeff's eyes widened. "I guess so," he grudgingly agreed.

"Oh, well there's your coworkers coming back." The deputy pointed down the hall toward Nurse Harper, who was returning to the nurses' station.

Jeff turned toward the direction the man was pointing and saw two nurses milling around. He also saw the other deputy waking up. "I was actually going downstairs."

"Oh," the deputy replied and stepped out of the killer's way.

Jeff walked back to the stairwell door and opened it. "See you later," he said before closing the door.

The killer wasn't going to be able to finish the job. He went back down the stairs, and when he reached the second-floor landing, the door opened. Before he knew it, he and the woman who had walked through it were face-to-face.

The nurse glared at the man. "Who are you?"

Jeff was surprised. The woman was staring at the ID badge on the lab coat, now facing outward.

"You're not—"

Jeff grabbed the woman before she could finish speaking and dragged her into the stairwell. He hit her once in the jaw and then tossed her over the railing to the basement floor, two flights down. He watched her hit the concrete floor, where she lay unmoving. "Damn!" he whispered. The killer rushed down the stairs and took the same route back out to the emergency room lobby. Jeff then hurried past the security guard and out to the parking lot, where he climbed back into his truck and took off the disguise. He beat his hands on the steering wheel just as his cell phone rang. He looked at the caller ID and sent Porter to voicemail again.

⁂

Senator Vince Livingston walked into his wife's bedroom after eight. He was tired and hadn't slept but for a few hours after leaving Frank's place. The monitor next to Linsey's bed flashed and beeped periodically. Fortunately for Vince, the lights and the beeps on the monitor told him his wife was still alive, and that was how he needed her, for a bit longer anyway.

"Hello, Senator," the nurse said in greeting.

Vince sat in his usual chair next to his dying wife. "Hello, how is she this morning?"

The nurse pursed her lips and put her hands on her hips. "About the same. No better, but no worse either."

"Good."

"Vince, is that you?" Linsey mumbled and opened her eyes.

Vince reached over and held his wife's hand. It was more for show for the nurse than sincerity. "Yes, how do you feel, my love?"

"Tired."

"Well, close your eyes and rest. I'll be right here when you wake up."

⁂

Brody had kept his word. The man had spent the early morning hours watching over the woman he had pulled from the South

Platte River, just as he had said he would. As the hour approached eight o'clock, the deputy stood close to the window staring out toward Pikes Peak. He had been there ever since the sun had begun its slow climb from behind the mountain. The snow that had come in from the late spring storm had melted from the roads, and only a few patches of white remained on the grassy areas of the mountain town. A few news station vans remained in the parking lot, likely hoping for more information about the woman behind him.

"Help me."

Brody spun around when he heard the woman's voice. He rushed to her bedside. "You're okay," he said in a soft, reassuring voice.

The mystery woman slowly lifted her head and looked around. "Where am I?"

"You're in a hospital. I'm Deputy Brody Katz with the Teller County Sheriff's Office. You're safe now," he said as he pressed the nurse's call button.

The patient closed her eyes, placed her hand against her forehead, and felt the bandages. "What happened to me?"

Brody didn't know how to answer her question. "I found you in the river and brought you here."

Nurse Harper came into the room. "Hello, I'm Nurse Harper. How are you feeling?" she asked as she checked the patient's vitals.

Brody took a step back and allowed the nurse to do her job. A few moments later, Doctor Dawson walked in. He took out a small light from his coat and leaned over the bed. "I'm Doctor Dawson. Can you look at me for a moment? I'd like to look at your eyes."

The patient turned toward the doctor. "What are you doing? What happened to me?"

Doctor Dawson shined the light into her eyes. "You have a head wound, and I'm using this light to see how your pupils adjust to it. It can tell me if you have something going on with your brain."

"Are they okay?" she asked once the doctor put the light back into his lab coat.

The doctor smiled. "They're responding just as they should."

"Can someone tell me what happened to me?"

Doctor Dawson and Nurse Harper turned and looked at the deputy. Brody's eyes went from one medical professional to the other. Finally, the deputy stepped closer to the bed.

Deputy Katz cleared his throat. "I can tell you what we know so far."

"Okay," she replied.

Brody stared into her green eyes for a moment. "All right, but first, can you tell me who you are?"

The question seemed to catch her off guard. She turned her head to the left and looked upward. Her eyes blinked rapidly. "I don't know," she whispered and put her hand on her head.

Doctor Dawson placed his hand on her shoulder. "That's okay. You've suffered a head injury, and it may take you some time to remember some things. Can you tell us what you do remember?"

The patient closed her eyes for a few seconds. "I remember running, falling, and then water."

The doctor turned toward Brody, who shrugged his shoulders.

"Can you tell me where you're from?" Brody asked.

Once again, the woman thought about it. "Am I from here?" she asked.

Brody shook his head. "We don't know, but I have some people coming by within the hour who might be able to help us."

"Okay," she replied.

"Are you hungry? We can get you some food," Doctor Dawson offered.

"I am. I think."

"Good," Doctor Dawson said and turned to the nurse. "Nurse Harper, can you get our guest something to eat?"

Harper smiled at the woman. "Absolutely. Now, you just try to rest, and I'll be right back."

The doctor started for the door but stopped short of walking out. He turned back toward Brody and signaled for the deputy to come into the hall with him.

Brody nodded that he understood, then stepped closer to the bed. "I'll be right back," he assured the woman before walking out.

Doctor Dawson stood just outside the patient's room. He had his arms crossed and his head down, and he appeared to be deep in thought when Brody joined him.

"I've heard of amnesia, but I've never seen anyone with it. What do you think?" he asked the doctor.

Doctor Dawson lifted his head. "Amnesia is real. Everything that we know she's been through can cause it. The sexual assault and other events of her victimization could cause post-traumatic amnesia. Post-traumatic amnesia could manifest aspects of retrograde amnesia, anterograde amnesia, or both. She could also have dissociative amnesia, which presents after suffering some kind of trauma."

"Is any one of them worse than the other?" Brody asked.

Doctor Dawson nodded. "Yes, the dissociative amnesia."

"Why?"

"Dissociative amnesia can cause someone to forget their identity and entire life until they awaken."

Brody had a blank expression on his face. "Kind of like she just did a few minutes ago."

"Exactly. If you guys can't identify her and no one recognizes her, we may never know who she is. Now, I have to make more rounds, but I'll be back around lunch to check on her again," Doctor Dawson advised and started to walk away.

"Doc, wait!" Brody said and reached out and grabbed the man by his arm.

"Yes, what is it?"

Brody turned toward the woman's door and then back to the doctor. "What do I tell her?"

"Nothing. She needs to come to terms with what's happened

to her. It's best if you don't overshare with her. If you think she can handle it, talk to her about your perspective of what happened. With any luck it might help trigger some of her memories. Again, just be careful not to overshare." Dawson offered and walked away to finish his rounds.

Brody didn't know what to do. He stood in the hallway until Harper walked up with two food trays.

"What are you doing out here?" the nurse asked.

Brody shrugged. "I don't know. I guess… I just don't know what to say to her," he confessed.

"No one is going to know what to say to her. Why don't we just go in there and talk to her? If she asks a question that we can answer, we answer it. It's better than leaving her in there alone," Harper suggested.

Brody's eyes widened, and he smiled. "I think that sounds like a plan. What's for breakfast?"

Chapter 3
Omelets

The mystery woman ate her breakfast while Deputy Katz explained how he had come to find her and where. The woman listened and occasionally asked questions that Brody had no answers to. Halfway through his cheese omelet, Brody saw the patient run her finger along the name tag taped on the metal lid that had once covered her breakfast plate.

"Jane Doe zero five three zero," she mumbled. She lifted her head and gave the deputy a quizzical expression.

"Jane Doe is used for anyone we don't know. The oh five three zero is the date I found you in the river," Brody explained.

"Anyone? Do you find a lot of Jane Does?" she asked.

"No. I've never found anyone like you while fishing," he quickly answered. The deputy didn't want to tell her the name Jane Doe was typically used for people who were unknown and deceased.

"Do you think I look like a Jane Doe?" she asked.

"No, not at all," Nurse Harper said, interjecting as she entered the room.

Brody turned toward the nurse and smiled. "I don't think she does either."

"Who do I look like then?"

Brody squinted and Harper pressed her lips together and both stared at the woman for a moment. Neither would tell the patient the truth about how she looked. Her head and arm were wrapped in bandages. Her legs, arms, feet, and face were scratched and bruised.

Brody was the first to say something. "Shannon," he suggested.

Harper shook her head from side to side. "Nooooo," she replied, in a tone that carried a lot of sass.

"Then who do you think, Harper?" the patient asked.

"I don't know, but I think the name needs to fit you for the moment."

Brody shook his head and shrugged his shoulders. "For the moment?"

Harper dropped her arms to the side. "Yes! Something like River, Deckers, or… I don't know, but it'll just be temporary until she gets her memory back."

Brody thought about it for a second longer, then came up with something. "I got it! How about Memory?"

Harper closed her eyes and thought about it for a moment. She opened them again, looked at the patient, and wrinkled her nose. "I think I like it!" she admitted.

The mystery woman grinned. "So do I."

"Well, Memory, how was your omelet?" Brody asked.

Memory's grin grew bigger. "To my recollection, it's the best I've ever eaten!" she proclaimed and laughed aloud.

Brody and Harper looked at each other and then laughed along with Memory.

Detective John Wilson entered the hospital a few minutes before nine. He found Doctor Dawson, who updated him on the patient's condition. A short time later, Detective Wilson entered the victim's room and saw Deputy Katz sitting in a chair next to the victim's bed, eating breakfast. The patient spoke to her nurse and didn't notice Wilson standing at the door, but Brody did.

Wilson nodded for Brody to come out into the hallway. Brody stood and was about to follow his friend out the door when he heard Memory speak.

"Brody, where are you going?" she asked.

The deputy turned and looked at her. "I'm just going into the hallway for a minute. I'll be right back."

Memory waited for Brody to leave the room before turning her attention back to her nurse. "What do you think of Brody?"

"I know he's been worried about you," Harper answered.

Memory raised one eyebrow. "I think it's his job to worry."

"Maybe, but it wasn't his job to stay here after he pulled you out of the river. He also volunteered to sit with you until you woke up again," the nurse replied.

"Again?"

Harper didn't think Memory remembered waking up earlier and stumbling into the hallway. "Yeah, you woke up earlier this morning, walked out of the room, and collapsed. Brody caught you before you hit the floor."

"I did?"

"Yes, and Doctor Dawson was worried that you would hurt yourself if you did it again. He wanted to restrain you to the bed. Brody and I, along with the other nurses, didn't like that idea and—"

"I don't think I would have liked that either," Memory blurted while rubbing her badly bruised wrists.

"Well, Brody volunteered to sit with you until you came around again," Harper explained.

Manuel woke up in the passenger seat of the Escalade and stared out the window. He took a moment to look at the countless windmills spinning in the fields on both sides of the road. He tapped Jorge, who was driving, on the shoulder. "How much farther?" he asked.

"Eight hours."

Manuel nodded and then turned around to look at Pablo,

loudly snoring in the back seat. "Sounds like he's calling pigs," the sicario leader whispered in Spanish.

"Maybe the fat one he liked at the bar the other night," Jorge whispered back.

Manuel laughed and then reached back and smacked Pablo's leg. "Wake up! Your hog's not coming!"

Pablo opened his eyes and glared at his boss. "What?"

"Where do you want to eat?"

"I don't care."

"Take the next exit, amigo. I need to piss and eat something." Manuel looked at his cell phone after hearing the text message sound. "Jeff Doyle," he whispered.

Detective Wilson waited in the hallway for Deputy Katz. He turned on the portable fingerprint scanner and checked to ensure it was working.

"It's Memorial Day weekend; how long will it take to get a match after you send her prints off to AFIS? Everyone's probably off," Brody commented after stepping into the hallway.

"Not long if she's in the system and people are working as they should be," the detective answered.

"I thought everyone was in the system if they had a driver's license. Memory's old enough to have a license," Brody replied.

"Memory?"

Brody took a deep breath and let it out. "Yeah, she didn't like being called a Jane Doe."

Wilson nodded. "Oh… Well, not every state employee puts them in correctly or makes sure they are readable."

"I hope she's in the system. Apparently, she has amnesia," Brody said.

Wilson nodded. "Yeah, I know. I spoke to Doctor Dawson a few minutes ago, and he told me."

"What happens if we can't identify her?"

"I guess she'll stay here until the hospital releases her. Then, we'll take her someplace safe until we can identify her," Wilson explained.

"Have you ever heard of something like this or worked any case like this one?" Brody asked of the man who had trained him when he had been hired.

Wilson shook his head. "I don't think anyone has."

Brody cleared his voice. "I didn't think so... Are you ready to go in?"

"Yeah, let's see if we can find out who Memory really is."

Harper and Memory were chatting away about the nurse's most comical situations she had experienced since becoming a nurse. When the lawmen entered the room, the women turned their attention to them.

"I'm Detective Wilson, and I'm working your case. I understand that you've lost your memory."

Memory sheepishly grinned. "I guess. I mean, that's what Doctor Dawson thinks anyway."

Wilson moved toward the bed and held the fingerprint scanner up for Memory to clearly see it. "I'd like to take your fingerprint, if that's okay."

Harper knew by the detective's behavior that he had been trained to work with victims of sexual assault.

"Yes, you can take them."

Wilson moved closer, slowly reached his hand out, and waited for her to place her hand into his.

"How does it work?" she asked.

The detective took her index finger and placed it onto the scanner. "You keep still, and I'll press this button on the side of the scanner. A light will slide across under the glass. It will collect an image of your fingerprint," he explained and activated the scanner.

Detective Wilson was patient and gentle while scanning all ten of Memory's fingers. When he had the last one, he stepped back, made sure he had an internet connection, and sent the fingerprints off to AFIS, the FBI's fingerprint database.

"Now, what do we do?" Memory asked.

"We wait," Wilson answered.

Brody sat in his chair next to the bed. "It sometimes takes a little while for it to come back."

Memory gave Brody a friendly smile. "Well, it's nice to have some company while I wait."

Wilson heard the beep from the scanner. "Sounds like we got a match," he proclaimed and looked at the scanner's digital screen.

Memory took a deep breath and asked. "Well, who am I?"

The detective lifted his head from the scanner. "It didn't come back. The scanner was beeping to let me know the batteries were low. I'll run back to the station and see if I can get it to come back quicker there," the detective answered and started for the door.

Brody saw the expression on his friend's face. He knew John was lying. "I'll walk you out." Brody followed John down the hall toward the elevator and waited until they were out of earshot from Memory's room. "What was that about?"

Detective Wilson surveyed the area around them before speaking. "I gotta see what happened to the scanner."

"Why? I heard it come back with a match," Brody declared.

"Yeah, it did."

"Then who is she?" Brody asked.

"I don't know, but she ain't Libby Smith, born December 26, 1934."

Brody stared at the ceiling, and John knew his old friend was adding the years in his head. "Eighty-seven."

"Yeah, eighty-seven," Wilson replied.

"Is the scanner broken?"

"I don't know, but I'm going back to the station to manually enter them into the computer. I'll come back before dinner and let you know what I find out," Wilson said as he started for the elevator with Brody following.

"Dinner? Why so late?" Brody asked.

The detective gave his friend a concerned expression. "A nurse was found at the bottom of the stairwell about an hour ago. We don't know anything about it yet. It could just be an accident. We've increased the number of deputies around the hospital. Still, until we know what happened, the sheriff doesn't want the press to know about it."

Brody turned and looked down the hall at the stairway door, then pointed at it. "That stairwell over there?"

"Yeah."

Brody tilted his head upward and pointed at the small half-moon shaped glass in the ceiling where a surveillance camera was installed. "What do the cameras show?" Brody asked excitedly.

Wilson shook his head. "I don't know. That's why I'm going down there right now."

"I'll come with you." Brody pressed the down button on the elevator.

"No, the sheriff wants you to go home, shower, and get some sleep."

Brody gave his friend a brooding expression. "I think I'm more useful with you."

Wilson knew Brody wouldn't just sit on the bench while everything played out. He also knew the deputy hadn't slept for more than a few hours or even showered since finding the woman. "Okay, you take the scanner, go back to the station, and enter her fingerprints manually. We'll meet back here at five o'clock and share what we've found out."

"That's a good idea… but how about I come back here just as soon as I get a hit on the fingerprints," Brody suggested.

Wilson looked at the floor and shook his head. "No, you'll enter her fingerprints, go home, shower, sleep, and then meet me back here at five, or you can just go home." John liked Brody, but if he wanted to be involved, it would be on John's terms.

Brody didn't like his friend's ultimatum, but he knew it was his only option. "Okay, five o'clock it is."

After leaving the hospital, Jeff drove back to the cabin where he had held the woman captive. The owner of the mountain retreat wouldn't be using it for another month, which provided the killer with a place to hide from Porter until he could figure out what to do. The hired gunman took an unopened bottle of whiskey from the cabinet, sat in the dining room, poured a shot, and thought about his options. Jeff knew Porter was most likely making other arrangements to kill the woman—and him. He had to figure something out and fast.

I could offer to give the up-front money back and finish the job for free, he thought as he poured another shot. He threw it back and slammed the glass onto the bar. "Damn it!" he shouted, took his cell phone out, and found Bret's number. Jeff knew what he needed to do, but it wasn't something he wanted to do.

"It's me. Are you available to help me move some furniture?"

"How heavy?" Bret asked.

"Very," Jeff replied and waited for the man to answer. "Did you hear me?" Jeff asked after a moment.

"Yeah, I can help for twenty-five."

Jeff wrinkled his forehead. He took the phone from his ear, stared out the window, and thought about it. Twenty-five thousand was all the up-front money he had been given, and it was half of the total for the job. It was also his only option. "Yeah, I'll pay it," he grudgingly agreed.

"Anything else?" Bret asked.

"We need to do it tonight, and you need to bring a suit," Jeff replied.

"Text me where you want to meet," Bret said and ended the call.

Jeff texted the cabin's address to the man, slid the phone across the table, and poured his last shot until after the job was complete. The killer laid down on the couch. He thought out a plan on how to get into the hospital. It took about an hour to work out all the details in his head, but he did it. There was a way to get to the girl and kill her, but many people could die.

I'll have to leave the country after this job is over. I'll need some traveling money for that, Jeff thought and went back to the dining room table. The contract killer picked his cell phone back up and called the man he had been avoiding.

Porter was waiting for the senator to finish his morning visit with his wife when his burner phone rang in the Livingstons' kitchen. He stared at the number before stepping into the living room. He peeked up the stairs and answered the call.

"You're kidding me, right?" Porter asked angrily.

"Shut up!" Jeff ordered. "I need more money."

Porter huffed. "Yeah, right!"

"No, you don't understand. I know who you work for, and I know this has something to do with him." Even though he wasn't positive, Jeff insinuated the job was for the senator. The hired gun figured he had nothing to lose by throwing out the bluff.

"How much?" Porter finally asked.

Jeff wasn't ready for his old friend to agree so quickly, so he knew the woman was a target worth a lot more than fifty grand. "Five hundred."

"Fine, but you need to finish the job first."

Jeff smiled. "I will tonight, but I want the money right after it's done. I'm leaving the country soon after."

"Yeah, I think it's best that we never see each other again. I'll have someone drive the money to you, but it's not getting delivered until I know the woman's dead."

Jeff knew that would be part of the deal. He had already thought about how to handle it. "It's a deal. I'll text you where I want to meet your guy when I'm ready for the money."

"All right," Porter replied and ended the call just as the senator came down the stairs.

After telling Memory he'd be back later, Brody made it to the sheriff's office and entered the fingerprints into the system just as Wilson had instructed him to. He drove home, showered, made a sandwich, and sat on his deck. The deputy enjoyed the snow-capped-mountain views to the west while also researching amnesia online.

Brody's cabin in the mountains of Colorado had been a dream of his ever since he had first been stationed at Fort Carson in Colorado Springs at eighteen years old. After twenty years in the Army, Brody retired, attended police academy at a local community college, and was soon hired by the Teller County Sheriff's Office. The lonely man bought a small fifth-wheel and parked it on the forty acres he had purchased ten years earlier. Brody's custom three-bedroom cabin, with its hardwood floors and wood cabinets built from reclaimed wood, took him a year to build. Now, he was surrounded by large evergreens, rolling mountains, the sounds of nature, and an incredible view of the Sangre de Cristo Range.

Brody's current situation in life was a dream come true—for a bachelor, anyway. The war on terrorism in the world's far corners had kept the man busy over the past twenty years. Unfortunately, Brody had seen his fair share of failed relationships over those years. Now, the only thing he longed for was the company of a woman who had a similar interest in the outdoors like him. Brody allowed his mind to drift back to thoughts of Memory for a moment. *She was beautiful,* he thought as his head began to fall forward. The deputy shook his head, stretched, and stood. "I need some sleep," he whispered.

After walking back into the cabin, Brody made his way to his bedroom, set his alarm, and laid himself on the bed. He dropped his head back, tucked his arms under his pillow, closed his eyes, and thought about the South Platte Floater. *How did she end up in the river? Who tried to kill her and why?* he asked himself. He fell asleep while a westerly breeze blew in through the window and across his body.

Chapter 4
Burgers

Detective John Wilson had not been able to interview the nurse found in the basement of the stairwell. Doctors had tried to stop the bleeding in her brain, but it had been in vain. After three hours of emergency surgery, the woman died. The detective hoped to review the hospital surveillance cameras but discovered they had started malfunctioning three months ago. No one at the hospital had bothered to schedule a service call.

The detective made his way back up to Memory's room at just before five, where he found Nurse Julia attending to the patient. "Can I come in?" he softly asked after peeking through the door.

"Yes," Memory answered.

"If you need anything, just press the call button," the nurse offered and walked out.

Detective Wilson stood next to the bed. He had questions but didn't know if the mystery woman could answer them. Still, they needed to be asked. "So, it's Memory for now?"

Memory smiled and shrugged her shoulders. "I guess it is, for now anyway."

Wilson smiled back. "I think it fits."

"That's what Brody and Nurse Harper said too."

Wilson nodded. "Great minds think alike. Now, if you don't mind, I'd like to ask you some questions if I could."

Memory sat straighter in the bed and placed her hands on her lap. "Absolutely, go right ahead. I'll try to answer them."

"Good. I'd like for you to close your eyes and relax," Wilson said as he sat in the chair next to the bed. He wanted to try a technique he'd heard about at an interview and interrogation seminar.

"Okay," Memory replied and closed her eyes.

Wilson cleared his throat. "Memory, I want you to take things real slow and tell me what you can remember."

The mystery woman took a moment and thought back as far as possible. "I remember running in the woods. There's snow. Someone was chasing me," she said as her eyes blinked quickly.

"Try to think back before that," Wilson encouraged.

Memory soon saw her hands in front of her. "It's dark. My wrists are in handcuffs. I have a wrench, and I'm hitting it on a metal pipe."

"Can you see anything else around you?"

"I… I don't know! It's so dark. I smell cigarette smoke. No, it's not a cigarette. A smoking pipe, maybe?"

The detective grew excited, thinking the victim was on the verge of a breakthrough. "What else is there? Do you smell, hear, or see anything else? What's around you?"

Memory pushed herself farther up the bed, as if she were trying to get away from someone. "He's coming!"

Wilson moved closer to the bed. He needed her to continue. "Who, Memory? Who do you see?"

"I don't see him… He's behind me, shouting about not being quiet!" Memory's voice began to tremble.

"You're okay," Wilson said softly.

"No… No… He's come back to hurt me again! He has a gun, and he's chasing me through the snow. No! Don't shoot!" Memory cried out and opened her eyes.

"You're okay, Memory." The detective reassured her as Nurse Julia rushed into the room.

"What happened? Her heart rate is way up!" the nurse asked as she checked her patient's vitals.

"We were going over what happened to her and—"

"With everything she's been through, I think it's too much right now!" the nurse replied in an angry tone.

Memory took a deep breath. "I'm okay. I just need a minute. What do you mean by, *with everything she's been through*?" she asked and looked at the detective for an answer.

John was at a loss for words. He knew she would have to be told about the sexual assault, but he wasn't ready to have that conversation with her. "Well…"

"John, I'm here!" Brody announced. He had walked in behind the nurse and heard what Memory had asked of the detective.

John turned and looked at his friend. "Hey, come on in," he uncomfortably said.

Brody greeted them with a smile. "Hello, Memory."

Memory's lips turned upward. "Hi, Brody," she replied.

Brody walked to the bed and held up a white paper bag. "I brought burgers."

"Oh, good! I had an unsavory turkey loaf for lunch." Memory glared at Nurse Julia.

"I don't make the food. I just deliver it," the nurse replied as she ran a cool cloth along the patient's forehead.

"Well, this is one of the best burgers you can get in town," Brody proclaimed as he removed one of the bison burgers from the bag and handed it to the patient in front of the nurse.

Nurse Julia knew that a burger and fries weren't part of her patient's meal plan. Still, she also knew she had misspoken earlier. "I'm going to the nurses' station, and I didn't see that food," the nurse said and walked out of the room.

"Is there one for me?" Wilson asked.

Brody gave his friend a disapproving glare. "Yeah, why don't you eat it in the hall while you check up on those fingerprints?"

Brody suggested as he pressed the bag hard against the detective's chest.

"Yeah, I think I will," Wilson agreed and hurried out of the room, leaving Brody and Memory alone.

Brody took his usual seat next to the bed. "It's just a bun with a buffalo patty in it. I had them put everything else on the side. We don't know if you even like cheese, tomatoes, onions, or lettuce. I also got a bunch of condiments," he offered as he dug through the bag for the tiny packets.

Memory was staring out the window. It seemed as though everything that had happened to her was starting to surface. "What happened to me?" She dropped her head and sobbed uncontrollably.

Brody placed the bag down, stood, and moved closer to the bed. He didn't know what to do, so he did what felt right. The deputy bent over and put his arms around her, and to his surprise, she wrapped her arms around him.

Memory squeezed him tightly as tears streamed down her face. "What did he do to me?" she asked between sobs.

The deputy closed his eyes and whispered in her ear. "He did what you're imagining he did," he confessed.

The mystery woman may not have known who she was, but she knew what had happened to her in the back of her mind, even if she couldn't remember it.

Lower Downtown Denver, or LODO as locals commonly referred to it, was crowded with people rushing into or out of one busy restaurant or another. Senator Vince Livingston had arrived early to '59ers and was seated in the Gold Rush room in the back, where he waited for her to arrive. His two bodyguards stood outside the private dining room, keeping an eye on anyone who got too close.

Lance tapped Porter on the shoulder and nodded his head

to the right. Porter looked past his partner and saw her walking toward them. Lance gawked at the woman. She wore a tight blue cocktail dress that left little to the imagination.

"Either I'm late or he's early," Kelly said after she walked up and stood in front of Porter.

Porter's lips turned downward. "He's early," he replied with a callous tone. The bodyguard didn't like Kelly, but the senator did, and that was all that mattered.

Kelly rolled her eyes. "Are you going to open the door for me or not?"

Porter stared at the woman, reached down, and started to open the door.

Kelly shook her head, stepped closer to him, and gently ran her hand along his cheek. She glared at the bodyguard and then leaned in close to his ear. "You're no better than me. We both take his money in exchange for whatever he desires. Trust me when I say your work is much dirtier than mine," she whispered and then lightly patted the man's face before walking into the room to join her date.

Porter felt his cell phone vibrating. He shut the door after the prostitute walked inside and answered the call.

"Yeah," he said.

"My guys are close. Where should they go? You haven't sent me the address yet," Frank Walters asked.

"Have them head west toward the town of Woodland Park. I'll text you the address," Porter replied and ended the call. He then texted Jeff's address to the drug dealer.

"Everything okay?" Lance asked.

Porter turned and faced the other bodyguard. "Yeah, I hope. How are you feeling?"

"I get dizzy sometimes, but the doc said it would pass," he admitted.

Porter smiled. "Good, I've got a bad feeling right now. I may need you later."

"What kind of feeling?"

Porter took a deep breath. "The kind where too many people are getting involved. Eventually, it'll be up to you and me to clear some of them out."

Memory spent twenty minutes letting it all out and coming to terms with everything that had happened to her. She knew nothing of her past, and she didn't care to remember the past few days either. The only thing she was sure of was the man sitting at the side of her bed eating cold fries from a bag. Deputy Brody Katz had pulled her from the brink of death, he had been there when she awoke, and he was there again.

"I ordered yours medium well. I didn't know how you'd like it," Brody admitted after watching her tear into the burger.

Memory smiled and wiped her mouth. "Neither do I. I mean, I could be a vegan for all I know."

"I haven't seen anything that would lead me to believe that you're a soymilk-drinking, legumes-and-nuts-eating vegan. Besides, after you tore into that burger, I think you must resign from the vegan club if you were one."

Memory put her napkin over her mouth and dropped the fry she'd had in the other hand back in the bag. "I'm sorry, I was so hungry!"

Brody laughed and stood. "I'm kidding," he said, then grabbed the fry and held it out for her to take.

Memory took the fry, placed it in her mouth, and made a playful growling sound when she bit into it. Her comical nature made Brody laugh once more. It also made him think about what he had read online concerning amnesia and the person's personality. "I have an idea," he happily declared.

Memory was caught off guard when he moved the chair from the side of the bed. "What?"

He took her dinner trash, placed it on the table, and took her by the hand. "Come with me."

"Okay," Memory replied as he led her into the adjoining bathroom, where he put her in front of the mirror.

"Who do you see?" he asked and stood back.

Memory stared at her reflection for a moment. She ran her fingertips along her cheekbone. "I look awful!"

"No, you don't. You're beautiful."

"Yeah, right! I have no makeup on, my hair is a mess, and my face is bruised," she replied before turning away from the mirror and dropping her head. "Why did you want me to do that?"

"Because now we know more about you," he answered.

She lifted her head and stared into his bright-blue eyes. "I don't understand."

"Well, from what I read about amnesia, a person's personality doesn't change. From what I can see, you have a great sense of humor, and you like to wear makeup and have your hair in some way that's not a mess."

Memory's eyes lit up. "What else can you tell?"

Brody took a step back, placed his hand under his chin, and looked the mystery woman up and down. "You're fit."

Memory glared at him. "I'm fit! Is that it?"

"Yeah, but that tells us things about you too."

"Like what?"

Brody took a few seconds to think before speaking. "You're here in Colorado, and many fit people live here. Maybe you're from here and are an outdoor enthusiast."

"What if I'm just here vacationing?"

"You could be, and come to think about it, you do have a nice tan," he replied.

Memory smiled once more. "Then it's settled. I'm from California! A beach girl!" she joked.

Brody laughed and nodded in agreement. "Sounds good to me."

Jimmy had arrived to work at three o'clock, and like many

nineteen-year-old security guards, he was already bored. He was sitting at the hospital's front desk, scrolling through the dating app on his phone, when two men in suits approached him. Jimmy stood, placed his phone in his pocket, and looked at the men. "Are you here to visit someone?"

Jeff glanced around the lobby. "Yeah, I'm Agent Ford with the FBI, and this is Agent Shepard. We're here to see the Jane Doe found in the river," he answered as he and Bret displayed their forged credentials.

All that Jimmy could focus on were the letters F–B–I next to the tiny gold badge. "Yes, sir. She's on the third floor. Room three oh six."

Jeff turned toward Bret. "Let's go," he said and started toward the elevator.

Bret followed but then stopped and looked back at the security guard. "Is she still being guarded?"

"Yes, sir. Two deputies are on the third floor. One at the stairwell door and the other at the elevator. There are more deputies roaming around the hospital. I also have a police radio if I need to call for backup. We have it all locked down. She couldn't be safer," Jimmy proudly declared.

Jeff had a thought. "Where's the security office? I need to review the footage from your surveillance cameras," he asked. The killer hoped to delete all the previous day's footage and to turn off the cameras before heading to the woman's room.

Jimmy frowned. "Our security cameras are not in operation right now. A deputy tried to view the footage earlier and found that there was a malfunction. We have someone scheduled to come by tomorrow."

That was the best news Jeff Doyle had heard since he took the job. "Good, it really needs to be working."

"Yes, sir. I've scheduled the repair myself and I'll make sure it gets done," Jimmy added.

Bret gave the guard a friendly grin. "We won't be long," he said and started for the elevator.

The two killers pressed the elevator up call button. When the doors opened, they got in, and Jeff pressed the button for the second floor.

"He said she was on three," Bret whispered.

Jeff looked at his hired man. "Yes, I know. You'll take the stairwell from the second floor to the third. The stairwell door has a window, so you'll see me get off the elevator. When I step off, I'll take the deputy at the elevator, and you take the deputy at the door."

"Then what?"

"Then we move toward the woman's room. Kill anyone at the nurses' station or in the hallway. We do this, and we do it quickly," he explained.

"You got it," Bret replied and then stepped off the elevator onto the second floor when the doors opened. He hurried down the hall toward the stairwell.

When the elevator doors closed, Jeff waited thirty seconds for Bret to get to the other end of the hall and into the stairwell before pressing the third-floor button. He reached to his side and pulled his 9mm from the holster. The killer retrieved the silencer from his pocket and screwed it onto the end of the barrel. *I gotta make this right and end it now,* he thought as he got ready.

In the stairwell, Bret pulled his .45 and attached his silencer to its end. He then hurried up the stairs taking two steps at a time. When he reached the third-floor door, the hired gun paused to peek through the window and saw the deputy sitting in a chair next to the door. He then looked toward the elevator doors at the other end of the hall, where the second deputy stood leaning against the wall. Bret checked his gun, kept his eyes on the elevator, and patiently waited for his employer to step onto the third floor.

Harper took a moment from updating her patients' charts to

look up at the detective, who was eating loudly. She thought he was good looking. "How's your burger? Sounds delicious," she politely yet sarcastically remarked.

Wilson almost choked. "It's good," he eventually answered with his mouth full.

"You know, you should slow down and take time to chew your food more before swallowing it."

Wilson grinned. "I'm sorry. I'm just in a hurry. I have the sheriff, the press, and the hospital pressuring me to find out who Memory really is. I keep getting the same information back on her fingerprints, and it's not her. So now I'm out of ideas and looking at a dead end."

Harper wrinkled her nose. "How do you know the fingerprints are not hers?"

Wilson pressed his lips together and then surveyed the area around them for anyone else who may be close enough to hear what he was about to say. "Her fingerprints come back to an elderly woman—and not just once but twice now. The woman in that room is anything but elderly."

"Sounds like a computer glitch, or someone entered the information incorrectly when either Memory's or the elderly woman's prints were first collected," the nurse suggested.

The detective wiped his mouth, took a long deep breath, and slowly blew it out. "Yeah, but I won't know until Monday. I called the FBI, and their person who can check the records by hand will be gone until then."

Harper huffed. "Seriously! Do they know that there's a woman who's a victim of who knows what waiting to find out who she is?"

"Yes, they do. But Memory's not their problem. She's mine," he declared as the elevator door chimed.

CHAPTER 5
VISITING HOURS ARE OVER

The doors to the elevator opened, and Jeff stepped out with his pistol at the ready. The deputy standing there was caught off guard, and before he could do anything, he was killed. The deputy sitting in the chair near the stairwell started to stand when the door behind him flew open, startling him. Bret moved into the hall and fired two shots into the deputy's head.

Both killers then started down the hallway.

Detective Wilson heard the elevator doors open and the sound of someone falling. He looked at Nurse Harper and stepped into the main hall from the nurses' station. "What the hell!" he shouted as he drew his pistol from his hip and fired it at the man coming down the hallway toward him.

Jeff and Bret fired their pistols at the deputy, hitting him in the shoulder and back. Detective Wilson fell to the floor and lay there on his back. Bret got to the lawman first. He aimed his pistol at the man's forehead and was about to pull the trigger.

"No!" Harper screamed.

Bret looked at the nurse, and he and Jeff raised their guns toward the woman and were about to shoot when suddenly the door to room 306 opened.

Brody hurried into the hall with his 9mm pointed outward. Both hired men spun toward him and found themselves in a two-way firing range with a trained shooter at the other end.

Brody was a combat veteran; he knew how to handle himself in a gunfight, and the two men who were trying to kill his friend were about to find out just how good he was. Brody fired at the man standing over John, first hitting him in the chest and leg.

Jeff was also hit in his chest, but his bulletproof vest stopped the bullet. He ran toward the nurses' station and took cover behind it but not before another bullet found the backside of his vest, where it was thinner. He winced in pain and dived toward the floor. Brody kept his aim on the man but stopped shooting when his target dropped behind the counter.

The deputy turned back toward the other shooter and found that he was no longer standing there. Bret had taken cover in a nearby room where he checked his wounds, waiting for Jeff to do or say something.

"You still up, bro?" Jeff shouted.

"Yeah, you?" Bret answered.

Brody kept looking back and forth from the nurses' station to the room door where the other man was taking cover. He then glanced at John, who, to his surprise, was alive.

"What do we do?" Bret yelled.

"He's alone. When I yell go, we both step out and take him," Jeff advised.

John rolled over and looked at the door and then back at Brody. He signaled that he would take the man hiding in the room. Brody nodded and took aim at the nurses' station.

Jeff nervously glanced around the area and saw the nurse hiding under the counter. He hurriedly crawled to her and grabbed her by the hair. "When I yell go, you stand with me, or I'll blow your brains out!" he threatened, in a tone that told Harper he meant what he said.

"Go!" Jeff yelled and stood while using the woman as a shield.

Bret stepped into the hall, but before he could do anything, the bullet from Detective Wilson's gun entered his head, right between his eyes. The gunman's knees buckled, and he dropped to the floor.

Brody didn't have a shot, so he took cover behind the corner of the wall. "Let her go, and you can walk out of here."

Jeff kept his gun pointed at the man behind the wall. He looked down the hall and saw Bret lying near the other cop on the floor. "I'm walking out of here, and no one better follow me! I'll kill her!" he threatened as he backed out of the nurses' station.

"Okay. Let her go!" Brody kept his gun on the killer as he moved down the hall.

"Drop it!" Jeff yelled and pointed his gun at the wounded man on the floor. He made sure to keep the nurse in front of him so Brody couldn't get a bead on him.

Detective Wilson realized the light around his eyes was getting darker. He dropped his gun and passed out just as the killer got close to him.

Jeff stepped over the downed detective. "I'm walking out the stairwell door, and you're not following. Besides, you need to take care of your friend."

Brody stayed behind cover but kept his pistol sight on the killer. "Let her go!" he ordered once more.

When Jeff got to the door, he looked through the small window, opened the door, and pushed the nurse forward. The last thing Brody saw was the top of the killer's head through the small window.

Harper rushed to Wilson and applied pressure to his wounds. Brody ran down the hall and opened the stairwell door, but it was no use. The killer was gone. He quickly checked the deputy by the stairway door but discovered he was dead. Brody ran to the other end and found the deputy by the elevator dead too.

"Brody, he's coming around!" Harper shouted.

Brody ran over and dropped beside his friend. "You'll be okay," he assured John.

The detective took a labored breath. "Take her someplace safe," he whispered and pointed back down the hall.

Brody turned around and saw Memory standing in the hallway. He looked at Harper and placed his hand on her shoulder. "Take care of him."

"I will! You take care of her!"

Suddenly, the stairwell doors opened. Brody took a shooting stance and aimed his gun at the door, only to see two armed hospital security officers stepping through it. "Damn!" he whispered. The deputy quickly concluded that the shooter must have gotten past them and was probably out of the hospital by now. Brody turned and ran to Memory. Right away he could see that she was in shock. "Let's go," he said. He then took her by the hand and started to pull her down the hall toward the elevator.

Memory jerked her arm from the deputy's grasp. "What happened?" she shouted.

Brody stopped and stared into her eyes. He needed to slow things down for her. "We're okay. Now, I need to take you somewhere safe," he said and softly took her by the hand.

Memory turned toward Harper, who was being joined by other hospital staff. All of them were working on Detective Wilson. When they reached the elevator, she stared at the deputy on the floor while they waited for the doors to open.

Brody stepped inside when the elevator opened and gently pulled Memory in with him. They took it to the basement, and when they got off, Brody hurriedly searched for some other clothes for Memory to put on.

"Where are we going?" she asked.

"To the only place I know that I can protect you. Please put these on," Brody answered as he handed her some surgical scrubs and slippers.

The scotch had a hint of vanilla and smoke. His office was warm, and soft jazz played from the room's speakers. Senator Livingston sat in his leather office chair behind his custom replica hand-carved Resolute desk, sipping the intoxicating beverage. He spent the afternoon reading over the final paragraph of a bill presented to the senate. When he finished reading it, he tossed it aside, drank the last sip of his scotch, turned the music off, and turned on the evening news.

As the senator walked to his liquor cabinet to pour another glass, he heard the news reporter say something that stopped him mid-step. Amanda Crosse was reporting on the murder of two deputies in the small mountain town of Woodland Park. The senator watched as police vehicles surrounded the local hospital.

"Damn it!" he shouted and threw his glass at the television screen, smashing them.

Porter, who had been in the kitchen also watching the news, rushed into the senator's office after hearing the crash.

The senator pointed at the cracked television screen where Amanda Crosse continued her broadcast. "What's this?"

Porter embarrassedly looked at his boss. "I don't know exactly."

"Well, find out, and I mean now!"

"Yes, sir," Porter replied before walking back out of the room.

Memory had followed Brody's instructions as ordered. She stayed low in the back seat of his Land Rover and didn't sit up until he told her it was safe. The drive from the hospital to the bumpy side road only took a few minutes. The dirt road to his cabin took longer, but eventually, they arrived at his mountain retreat. Brody spent most of the afternoon on the phone with Sheriff Kendrick. Memory sat on his couch, watching the news coverage about the shooting at the hospital.

After nine o'clock, Brody walked into the living room and sat in his recliner across from his houseguest. Memory picked up the remote and muted the television.

"So, what now?" she asked.

Brody could tell she was still shaken by the events of the day. He leaned forward and smiled. "First, tell me how you're doing?"

Memory started shaking her knee nervously. "I'm okay, I think—It was a lot. I was scared and still am but not as much as I was."

Brody knew the events at the hospital were traumatic for anyone to deal with and even more for someone like Memory, who had already suffered so much already. "Well, it looks like you get to spend the next few days with me."

"Why? I mean, shouldn't we go to a—"

"Safehouse?" Brody interjected before standing and walking into the adjoining kitchen.

Memory watched Brody open the refrigerator door. She was waiting for him to say something else, but he didn't. He just took out two beer bottles and walked back into the living room. The deputy twisted off the top of one bottle and handed it to her, sat back down in the recliner, and twisted the other one open.

"I spoke to the sheriff, and he said my place was the best safehouse he knew of. He also spoke to Doctor Dawson, who said I was to watch you for anything out of the ordinary," Brody explained.

"Is that it?" she asked.

"No, the doc says you can start eating a regular diet, and after the day we've had, beer is part of that diet," he added and took a long drink.

Memory couldn't do anything but shake her head and smile. "Do I even like beer?" she asked rhetorically and then took a long drink as well.

"Well, it's not one of those fancy craft beers, but it'll work in a pinch."

Memory's eyes watered, and she put her hand over her mouth. "I like beer!" she blurted.

Brody laughed, and Memory did the same. The hours seemed to pass quickly, and while her host made a late-night dinner, Memory sat on the deck wrapped in a blanket, watching the moon slowly drift upward from behind the mountains.

"I hope you like lamb chops and macaroni and cheese," Brody said as he carried two plates out of the house and placed them on the table.

Memory walked over and sat at the table. "It smells wonderful. I'm sure it'll be fine."

"I hope so," he replied and went back inside. Brody grabbed a bottle of wine and two glasses.

Memory watched him place a wine glass in front of her and start to fill it up. "Wine! How romantic," she said jokingly.

Suddenly it came to Brody. "Oh, I just thought a glass of wine would be good with the chops. I didn't mean to—"

Memory laughed. "It's okay. Please fill her to the top," she said encouragingly as she held her glass up and out toward him.

Brody smiled. He had been right about her having a good sense of humor. He filled her glass, then his, and sat next to her. "Let me know if you'd like me to cook it a little longer."

"All right. You know, earlier I was rude," Memory admitted.

Brody gave her a surprised expression. "Rude—rude, how?"

Memory put her fork and knife down. "I was more concerned about myself, and I should have asked how Detective Wilson and the others were, but I didn't. I'm sorry for that. Do you know how they're all doing?"

Brody took a drink of wine and placed the glass down. "There's no need to apologize. You've been through a lot, and you're still going through it."

"I know, but they were hurt protecting me. Are they okay?"

"John is recovering from his surgery. The two deputies are still in surgery," Brody answered, but it wasn't all true. John Wilson was recovering from his surgery. The two deputies had died, but that was something he didn't think Memory needed to know just yet.

Memory cut a bite of the white meat. "Good! You call him by his first name. Is Detective Wilson a friend of yours?"

Brody nodded. "He is now."

"He is now. Well, that sounds like a story about the two of you," Memory said and took a drink.

The deputy looked upward. "I guess it is."

"Don't keep me in suspense. Do tell."

Jeff made it back to his employer's cabin and immediately poured himself a drink. He didn't know what to do, where to go, or who to call. The only thing he knew to do was to continue to ignore the countless calls from Porter Rollins. Jeff knew he was a dead man if Porter—or anyone else he decided to hire—found him. He also figured that the deputy and the others had gotten a good look at him earlier. He believed he had mere hours before everyone looking for him finally found him. As the hour approached ten o'clock, the hired killer was drunk, tired, hurt, and Porter was calling once more, to make matters worse. Jeff looked at his phone, took the call, and shouted obscenities. The killer then stumbled over and fell onto the couch. It was done. He would be leaving the country in the morning.

"Mexico bound!" he slurred, then dropped the whiskey bottle to the floor and passed out.

Porter and Lance had been relieved by the midnight shift. Now, the two men sat in Porter's apartment, waiting for Jeff to answer his phone. After Jeff finally answered the call and yelled at Porter, the man sat there staring blankly out his patio window.

"What do you want to do?" Lance asked.

Porter turned toward his partner. "Do you still have that guy who can track a phone?"

Lance nodded. "You mean Willy? Yeah, I can call him, but he'll want to be paid."

"How much?"

"At least five grand," Lance answered.

"All right. Make the call and give him this number." Porter

held his phone up for Lance to see Jeff's number.

The dinner plates were washed and put away. Memory was relaxing on the couch and reading a book she'd found on Brody's bookshelf. Her host stood outside on the deck, on the phone. He was speaking to Sheriff Kendrick again. After dinner, the deputy had spent most of the evening on the phone with either the sheriff or someone else from the sheriff's office.

"How are you doing?" Brody asked after walking back inside.

Memory looked up from the book. "I'm doing okay. What's the latest?"

Brody moved closer to her. "Well, staying here hasn't changed. The sheriff has put deputies on my road a little way up from the main road, where they won't be seen."

Memory walked to the window and gazed into the darkness. "Can anyone get here another way? Maybe from another road?"

Brody walked over and stood behind her. "The road we came in on is the only way up here. We're surrounded by the Pike National Forest. It would be a long hike to get here. The only other cabin is about ten miles away," he explained and headed for the deck. "Come out here, and I'll show you something."

Memory followed him outside, where he uncovered a telescope. She watched as he turned it to the east and spent a few minutes turning the knobs on its sides.

"Take a look," he offered and stepped back.

Memory moved forward, placed her right eye to the eyepiece, and saw a cabin with its lights on. "Wow! That's ten miles away?"

"Yes."

"Now let me show you something else," Brody suggested. After Memory moved back, he repositioned the telescope. Again, he adjusted the knobs and stepped back.

Memory looked at him suspiciously but stepped back up to the telescope. "What? Wait! Is that a man smoking a cigarette?"

"Yes, that's Deputy Jackson. Well, I think it's Jackson anyway. He and another deputy are guarding the road to my place."

"I'm glad they're there."

Brody chuckled. "Yeah, me too."

Memory straightened from the spyglass and turned to face her host. "Do you think I could take a shower or a hot bath?"

Brody nodded. "Yeah, come on, and I'll show you where it is," he said and walked back inside, with Memory right behind him.

The bathroom he led her to was off the master bedroom. The bathroom had a tan-and-beige tile floor with similar-colored tile around the jacuzzi tub. Memory walked in and stood on the small carpet square in the bathroom's center. "It's really nice. Did you decorate it?"

"Yes, I built the cabin and finished everything inside," Brody replied.

"Well, you did a great job," she said and looked at herself in the mirror. "Oh, look at me. I'm a mess!"

"Nah, you look… um…" Brody quickly found himself at a loss for words.

Memory rolled her eyes and bit her lip. "Yeah, right. Now, get out of here and let me get to work."

Brody stepped out of the bathroom and shut the door behind him. He stood there for a minute and remembered that his sister had left some clothes in the guest bedroom when she and her family had visited last summer. *They're about the same size,* he thought.

Chapter 6
Late-Night Visitors

Memory turned on the water to fill the tub and then stood in front of the mirror. She removed the bandages from around her head. She pulled the longer hairs from the top of her head back from the right side. There, she found the side of her head had been shaved. She also found a long wound with dried blood around it that had ten staples keeping it closed. A tear formed in the corner of her eye that eventually found its way down her cheek. Memory covered her mouth and let out a muffled sob. After a moment, she unwrapped her arm and examined the bullet wound there. Finally, she removed the baggy surgical scrubs, stepped backward, and stared at her bruised and battered body. "You'll be okay," she told herself.

Memory stepped into the tub, eased herself into the hot water, and pushed the button for the jacuzzi jets to come on. She allowed herself to be taken away from it all, for a little while anyway.

Brody found his sister's clothes in the guest bedroom's closet and took them back upstairs. He laid some of them out on the bed for Memory to choose from. He then went back into the living room and called the hospital.

"Third floor nurses' station. This is Harper."

Brody smiled when he heard Harper's voice. "Nurse Harper, it's Deputy Katz."

"Deputy Katz! How's my patient?" the nurse excitedly asked.

"She's okay. How's Detective Wilson?"

"He's stable, but he's not out of the woods yet."

Brody swallowed hard. "Are you going to be there all night?"

"No, I'm actually not here now. They sent me home after the shooting, and I just returned after my friend, who is on duty, called and told me he was out of surgery."

"All right. Can you have your friend call me when or if anything changes?"

"Yeah. Is the number that came up on the caller ID the one she should call?"

"Yes."

"Okay, I'll make sure you get a call."

"Thank you."

Harper looked around the nurses' station. "I'm going to text you my number. If you guys need anything, call me," she offered.

"Okay."

The three sicarios followed the directions up the dirt road. The cartel soldiers didn't know what to expect when they arrived. All they knew was that they were to meet a man named Porter, and they were to help him with whatever he needed done.

"Who is this Porter?" Pablo asked from the back seat, where he was checking the action on his 9mm.

Manuel was loading one of the magazines for his .45 in the passenger seat. He looked back at Pablo for a second and went back to loading another magazine. "I don't know. Frank says we're to help this man Porter, so that's what we do."

Jorge found a place to park in the woods that was out of view of the cabin. "This looks like a good spot."

Manuel lifted his head and surveyed the area. "Yes, turn off the engine."

Jorge did as he was told and started to get out. Manuel grabbed him by the arm. "Make sure you stay out of sight. I don't want this Porter to know there's three of us until I'm ready to let him know."

"Okay," Jorge replied and got out of the car.

"Pablo, you come to sit up front," Manuel ordered.

It wasn't long before the three men saw a car's headlights coming up the dirt road.

The spring night air was cool, and a full moon sat high. Brody was in a wooden chair on his deck, enjoying the peace and quiet that only the mountains of Colorado could provide, while a small fire burned in his clay chiminea. He thought about having another drink but remembered he was on duty and not on vacation. The drinks earlier in the evening had probably been a mistake. He needed to stay on point from here on out. The soda sitting on the table next to him was a better choice for the witness protection detail he'd found himself working.

"It's cold out here," Memory announced as she stepped out onto the deck.

Brody jumped up and stared at the woman standing before him. She no longer wore oversized hospital scrubs, her bandages were gone, and her hair was down. The pajama bottoms and T-shirt he had laid out for her fit better than he'd thought. "You look much better," he said.

"Thank you. I wanted to save the jeans and other clothes for tomorrow. I thought these were better for tonight. Besides, this may not be appropriate to wear if someone stops by tomorrow," Memory explained while pulling at the T-shirt and looking at the words written across the front of it.

The deputy snickered after seeing the phrase. "At least the other girls will know," he joked.

Memory read the phrase aloud. "Sorry girls, I'm taken."

"It was hanging up with my sister's other clothes. It belongs to Joe, my nephew. He's twelve. I bought it for him last summer," Brody embarrassedly admitted.

Memory smiled and sat in the chair next to his. "So you're one of *those* uncles."

"Those uncles?" Brody asked as he added a log to the chiminea.

"Yeah, the kind of uncle that spoils his nephew. Let me guess, you probably bought Joe too much candy when he was a baby, loud toys when he was a toddler, and loud music now that he's about to be a teenager. I can only imagine what goes through your sister's mind every time her son opens a gift from his uncle."

Brody pressed his lips together and grinned. "Yeah, I guess I am one of those uncles."

"I knew it!" She pulled her legs close to her body and wrapped her arms around them.

Seeing she was cold, he hurried back inside, grabbed a blanket from the coat closet, and gently laid it around her shoulders.

Memory looked up into his eyes. Neither one of them said anything for a moment. "Thank you," she finally said, breaking their silence.

Porter and Lance found the cabin easily, using the address Willy had given them for the location of the cell phone trace. They also found Manuel and Pablo waiting for them. Porter pulled his pistol from the holster and held it in his lap as they approached the sicarios. He had never worked with the cartel, nor had he ever had a reason to do so, until now. When Lance saw his partner pull his pistol, he did the same and laid it between his legs. He then pulled the sedan to the side of the road, shut the lights off, and looked to Porter for instructions. Suddenly, one of the men in the other car got out and started to walk toward them.

"I'll get out and meet him. You cover me from back here," Porter ordered and put his gun back in his holster.

Lance opened his door but didn't get out. "I got you covered. If you must run, run to the right, into the woods. Make your way back to the road and wait for me at the last intersection we drove through."

"All right," Porter replied, then got out and headed toward the other man.

"Porter." Manuel spoke in a thick accent.

Porter stepped closer. "Yeah, you Manuel?"

"Yes," the sicario leader answered and stepped forward, until he was directly in front of Porter. He extended his hand.

Porter reached out and shook it. "Do you know what to do?"

"No, my employer just told me to meet you here, and you would explain. I'm sure whatever you need our help with involves killing someone inside the cabin," Manuel answered.

Porter nodded. "It does."

"How many inside?"

"One for sure, but there could be more. The man you're to kill doesn't live here."

Porter shook his head. "No, he doesn't."

Manuel rubbed his forehead and stared down at the road. He then turned and motioned with his arm for Pablo to join him. To Porter's surprise, a third man stepped out of the woods onto the road, right next to the passenger side of Lance's car.

"What the—" Lance immediately brought his gun up.

"Easy, amigo. We're all on the same team," Jorge said while holding his hands in the air.

Porter quickly turned around. "It's okay, Lance!"

Lance put his gun away and glared at the man.

"We'll need a plan," Manuel stated.

"Then let's make one," Porter suggested.

Manuel turned and looked down the road at the dimly lit cabin. "This man, who is he?"

"Nobody," Porter answered.

After midnight, the last log in the chiminea burned down to nothing more than a few brightly glowing embers among a pile of ash. Brody looked at his beautiful houseguest, who appeared tired yet comfortable wrapped in the blanket.

"A penny for your thoughts," she said when she discovered him staring at her.

Brody shook his head from side to side. "Tired. Really tired." He stood and stretched. "Maybe we should get some sleep."

"I agree. Where am I going to sleep?" Memory stood and started folding the blanket.

"My room," he answered.

She tilted her head to the side and gave him a playful expression. "Your room?"

Brody squinted and scratched the back of his head. "I mean that you can stay in my room, and I'll sleep in one of the others."

Memory stepped closer to him. "Nope. I can't have that. I can sleep in one of the other rooms."

Brody closed his eyes and shook his head from side to side. "No. Look, they all have king-size beds and adjoining bathrooms. My bathroom is just a little nicer, and besides, all your new clothes are already in there," he said happily. The trained soldier purposely didn't tell Memory that the master bedroom was safer and easier for him to defend. Brody didn't know if the men who were after her would be able to find her, but if they did, he needed to be ready.

Memory smiled. "All right. I guess I'll sleep in your room. I don't think you're going to let me win this argument."

"Not a chance," Brody replied and took the blanket from her

hands. "Now follow me, if you would please."

"Right behind you, sir."

The sicarios, all in their tactical gear, quietly stepped through the woods, making sure they stayed hidden within the shadows of the trees as they approached the cabin. If Manuel had had a choice, any night other than one with a full moon would have been better. As he got closer, the leader squeezed the mic on the front of his vest. "Are you set?" he asked and waited for his men to respond.

Jorge stood ready at the front door, and Pablo was at the door on the side of the house. Porter and Lance remained out by the road, in case the man inside got out of the cabin.

"Ready," Jorge said and adjusted his bulletproof face shield.

"Pablo ready."

"We're all set," Porter said into the mic.

It was now or never. Manuel sprinted from the tree line to the side of the cabin. He wedged a screwdriver between the metal panel door and its frame. After a few seconds and a lot of pressure, the metal latch on the door broke free. A loud metallic pop accompanied it.

Jeff was still asleep when something woke him. He lay there on the couch, not moving. After a few uneasy seconds, he secured his pistol from the coffee table and quietly checked to make sure it was loaded. A few more seconds later, he heard the deck boards on the front porch of the cabin squeak. *Someone's outside!* he thought and rolled off the couch, ensuring he stayed low. Quickly but quietly, he crawled to the chair where his bulletproof vest lay. "I may need this again," he whispered as he slid the heavy vest over his head. He secured it around his torso and crawled to the dining room, where he hid under the sizable oval mahogany table. "Let's do this," he whispered as he took aim at the front door and mentally prepared himself for an attack.

"Damn it!" Manuel fumbled with the breaker box. Using his cell phone's flashlight, he found the main breaker and put his thumb and index finger on it. "Get ready!" he ordered into the mic.

Jorge stepped in front of the door and set himself up to kick it open. Pablo did the same at the side door.

Jeff kept his eyes on the front door when the kitchen, office, and hall lights went off. The experienced gunman never took his eyes or gun off the front door. He waited until the intruder entered the cabin before shooting him in the chest and face when it burst open.

Jorge was thrown off when he felt the round hit his chest— and the second one that bounced off his face shield. He quickly dropped to a knee just as Pablo rushed through the side door.

Jeff flipped the dining room table over and took cover behind it while the two intruders used their MP5s to fill the expensive table full of lead. Two rounds found their way through the wood and into the back of Jeff's vest. He fell forward, but then he heard what he had been waiting for. The shooter at the door dropped his magazine and was reloading. Jeff stood and ran at the man, firing his 9mm rapidly at the intruder, but he wasn't going down.

When Jorge had his gun reloaded and ready, he felt the target's hand on his Kevlar helmet as he yanked his head backward. He then felt the hot barrel of the man's gun under his chin.

Jeff pulled the trigger, sending a bullet through the hitman's head. He then took the hitman's MP5 and shot at the intruder who had come in through the side door.

Pablo stood his ground. He moved forward, firing at the man who had just killed his friend. He didn't stop until he felt the hot metal that entered his thigh just above his knee. He dropped to the floor and hid behind the table his target had used.

Jeff saw another opportunity and took it. He ran for the back deck, firing the MP5 at the glass door, then crashed through it. He ran toward the railing just as Manuel entered the house.

"Damn!" Manuel shouted and fired at the back of the man as

he jumped off the side of the deck. Manuel ran out and stood at the railing and fired blindly into the dark timber. "He got out and ran out behind the cabin!" he yelled into the mic.

Porter threw the radio on the ground and pounded his fist against the tree beside him.

Lance walked up to him and asked, "What do we do now?"

Porter's face was etched. "I don't know. Let's go in and see if there's anything we can find that'll help."

Manuel went into the cabin and looked at Jorge's body. He lifted his head and surveyed the area for his other man. "Pablo!"

"Here. I'm here," Pablo answered.

Manuel walked over and knelt beside his old friend. Pablo was doing everything he could to stay awake. The man's blood was pooling around him. The bullet that had ripped through his thigh had severed his femoral artery.

"I'm not going to make it, my friend," Pablo whispered.

Manuel removed his helmet and placed his hand on Pablo's shoulder. "It was a good ride, amigo."

"Yes, very good," he replied and then took his last breath.

Porter rushed into the cabin and found the dead sicario near the front door. He scanned the room and saw Manuel kneeling next to his other man. "We gotta go," he said quietly.

Manuel glared at the man. He then walked over and stood in front of him. The sicario leader was angry, and Porter knew it. "This man is not a *nobody*. How is it that you know of him?"

Porter took a deep breath and slowly blew it out. "He and I were Navy SEALs together."

Manuel closed his eyes, shook his head from side to side, and chuckled before walking over Pablo's body. He stood over his fellow soldier, then turned and glared at Porter. "Don't you think that's something you should have mentioned earlier?"

"I thought we'd catch him off guard," Porter replied.

Manuel turned his head upward and thought before speaking. He then turned toward Porter once more. "We? You and your man were outside. My men and I came in here after a *nobody*!

71

A *nobody* who was a trained operator." Manuel stepped closer to Porter. "A *Navy SEAL* and a *nobody* are two very different targets!" Manuel shouted and started to walk out of the cabin.

"Would you have changed your plan?"

Manuel stopped short and slowly spun back around toward Porter. "Yes, I would have had you and your man enter the cabin with my men."

Manuel walked out to his vehicle, opened the trunk, and took out a gas can. He then started back toward the cabin. Porter and Lance watched him.

"What do you plan on doing with that?" Porter asked.

Manuel did not look back as he walked toward the cabin. "Destroying the evidence," he answered as he unscrewed the gas cap.

"Then what?" Porter called.

Manuel turned around and gave Porter a determined expression. "We find this *nobody,* and we kill him."

Chapter 7
Cold

The Christmas tree was decorated beautifully, holiday music played from the speakers, and many presents were spread out under the tree. A little girl stood on the couch, watching the snow fall outside from the cabin's living room window. She wore a floral lace and solid red festive dress that ran the entire length of her body. Her long blonde hair was perfectly curled and fell over her shoulders. She clung to an expensive doll that resembled her in both appearance and dress. The woman in the car in the driveway had given the girl the doll right before they'd had their picture taken together. She waved at her father as he stood in the snow next to the car. He and the woman waved back.

Suddenly, the little girl was no longer a child looking out a large cabin window. She was now a grown woman, sitting naked on a cold concrete floor. The sound of metal on metal rang out. *Please help me,* she heard herself cry out. Then there was the smell of alcohol and smoke on a man's breath. She heard him shout, "Why can't you just be quiet?"

"No, No!" Memory screamed as she sat up in bed. She was covered in sweat, and her heart was racing. The room was dark, and as she tried to collect herself, she heard the man's voice repeating the same words. Memory scooted herself back against the headboard and pulled her legs close to her. She rocked back and forth and tried to recall the little girl's memory of looking out the window.

＊

Jeff Doyle woke to the sound of sirens blaring. He jumped from the bunk and hurried to the window with his gun at the ready. He peered out the window toward the dirt road and caught a glimpse of the fire truck speeding past. He let out a sigh of relief, sat on the bunk, and grimaced in pain. He had escaped the cabin and the leap from the back deck, but not without injury. The man shooting at Jeff as he'd left the cabin had been successful. One bullet from the shooter's gun had passed through the meaty flesh above his left shoulder, taking a large chunk of Jeff's muscle and tissue.

The tiny hunter's cabin was about two miles from the cabin he had been staying in, and it was the first place he had come to where he could collect himself after the attack. There was no running water, electricity, or comfort that the other cabin had afforded. However, it was concealed from the service road by large trees, it had a few old handmade bunks with thin mattresses on them, and there were some worn-through blankets he had found in a closet that he used to keep warm.

As he examined his injury, he thought about what he needed to do next. He couldn't return to the other cabin or wait it out. Jeff needed to get moving, and he needed to get moving fast. The problem was that he had no vehicle to get out of the woods with. He used an old, stained washcloth to cover the wound and then lay back and thought about what to do. After a few minutes, he remembered the hiking trail three or four miles away. *By the time I get there, someone will be hiking the forest—someone who drove to the hiking trail,* he thought as he closed his eyes and applied pressure to his wound.

At seven thirty, Brody awoke. He was lying on his right side, and he was cold. He reached behind him with his left hand and felt for his comforter but felt something hard. Brody quickly turned over, sat up, and found Memory sleeping soundly next to him. He smiled and just sat there for a few minutes, watching her. Brody didn't know why she had come into his room during the night, nor did he care. She was wrapped in his warm comforter and appeared at peace.

He finally got out of bed at about eight o'clock without disturbing his very own Goldilocks. Brody went around the cabin, checking the doors and windows with his gun in hand. The deputy then walked out onto the deck, uncovered the telescope, and pointed it at the road. He saw two new deputies standing guard. After he was satisfied the area was secured, he walked into the master bathroom, turned on the shower, and undressed.

Brody was about to open the shower door when he noticed there wasn't a clean towel. He stepped toward the linen closet and opened it but remembered he had done laundry before going fishing the other day. The clean towels were still in the dryer. Brody grabbed the only towel from the closet. It was thin, ripped, and ragged, to say the least. He tied it around himself anyway and walked into the living room as he headed for the laundry room. He peeked into the other bedroom and saw Memory still sleeping. He then tiptoed down the stairs and walked into the laundry room, where he took the clean bath towels out and folded them. After a few minutes, he headed back upstairs, carrying a large bundle.

"Good morning," Memory said cheerfully as her host walked into the master bedroom.

Brody was surprised. He quickly stepped back, dropping the clean linens to the floor and the towel that covered him. "Shit!" he blurted. He reached down, picked up his towel, and wrapped it around himself. "Good morning," he awkwardly greeted.

Memory smiled, looked down, and then quickly looked up at the ceiling. "Your towel seems to have a hole in the front there," she said as she pointed downward.

Brody's eyes widened. He knelt and grabbed another towel. "I was—"

"About to get in the shower?"

"Yes," he answered.

"I'll be in the kitchen," she said as she hurried past him on her way out of the room. However, curiosity got the better of her. She turned and took a quick peek at his bare backside. *Nice,* she thought before closing the door behind her.

Brody stood there, embarrassed. Once again, he bent down to pick up the clean towels, but the towel around his waist dropped to the floor. He stood naked and frustrated. He kicked the towels toward the bed.

Then without warning, the bedroom door opened again. "I found some eggs and sausage. Do you like—" Memory had caught the deputy by surprise once again. She turned away and quickly shut the door.

This time, Brody didn't try to cover himself. He just stood there shaking his head. "Cook whatever you like," he yelled before walking into the bathroom.

The expensive cabin was partially burned. Two of the outside walls were completely missing. The other two still stood but barely. The Woodland Park Fire Department had responded to the blaze after some campers had spotted the flames through the trees. As the firefighters had walked through what was left of the cabin, they'd found the remains of two people under some charred debris. The fire chief called the sheriff's office, and a short time later, Deputy Perkins arrived.

"What do you think?" the fire chief asked.

Perkins didn't answer him at first. He was standing in the middle of what remained of the cabin, staring down at the burned corpse.

"Deputy Perkins, did you hear me?"

"Yeah, make the call. I think we need an arson investigator. I'll call the sheriff and everyone else," Perkins finally answered.

"You think this is a homicide?"

A cool breeze blew across the scene, and the stench of burned flesh filled the air. The deputy covered his mouth and nose. "Maybe, but that's not my call."

The rental was just outside of town, and Porter had paid for it from a private account that the senator had set up overseas. He had planned for only him and Lance to be staying there until they were finished with the job, but they had an additional guest. Porter and the other two men had slept for about four hours before getting up and working on finding where Jeff Doyle and the woman were. Nothing had changed. Both needed to die—and soon.

Manuel walked in and found Porter sitting at the dining room table, drinking a cup of coffee. "What's your plan to find this man?"

Porter didn't like sharing the rental with the sicario, but he had no other options. Frank had ordered it, and since the entire mess, from the beginning, was his fault for hiring Jeff Doyle, he was in no position to argue. "I don't have one."

Manuel poured himself a cup. "What of the woman?"

Porter wrinkled his forehead. "No plan with her either."

"Then what are we to do?"

"I'm going into town to have a look around. Woodland Park is a small town, and people in small towns tend to talk."

Manuel nodded in agreement. "What am I to do?"

Porter reached into his pocket and took out a sheet of paper.

"This is where Jeff Doyle lives. Why don't you and Lance stake it out and see if he returns?"

Manuel took the paper and read the address. "Okay, we'll meet back here later and discuss our next step."

By the time Brody stepped out of the shower, the smell of breakfast had drifted throughout the cabin. He quickly dressed, hurried out of the bedroom, and found Memory standing at the stove in the kitchen.

"Smells good," he announced as he walked in and stood behind her.

Memory turned around and smiled at him. "I don't know what to say. I can cook!" she happily declared. She pointed at the chair at the end of the table. "Sit down and eat."

"All right," he said and took a seat in front of a plate covered with eggs and sausage links.

"I wish I could explain it, but I can't. I just turned the stove on and started cooking," she said and sat in the chair next to Brody.

"It's probably muscle memory." Brody took a bite of eggs.

Memory raised her brow. "What?"

"Muscle memory. I read about it when I looked up amnesia," he explained and took another bite.

Memory's eyes widened. "What else did it say?"

"Well, when someone has amnesia, they sometimes can remember how to do certain things based on muscle memory," he clarified and took yet another bite.

Memory tilted her head and squinted one eye. She didn't quite understand, and Brody knew it.

"Have you ever heard the phrase *'it's like riding a bike'?*"

"I think so," she answered.

"Okay, apparently, we remember certain things we do repetitively and—"

"Like brushing my hair, cooking food, washing, and other things like that!" Memory said excitedly.

Brody grinned. "Exactly," he agreed right before answering his ringing cell phone.

Memory ate her breakfast while Brody spoke to someone on the phone. She could tell by the concerned expression and his unblinking gaze on her that whoever it was on the other end of the phone call, their conversation concerned her. After a few minutes, Brody finished the call and stared at his houseguest.

"Was that about me?" she asked.

Brody sat back in his chair with arms crossed, took a deep breath, and slowly blew it out. "Yes, the sheriff wants us to come into the office at eleven. He's bringing in a specialist to see you."

Memory took a sip of coffee. "What kind of specialist?" she asked.

"Someone who knows more about amnesia, I guess."

Memory stared down at her plate at the sausage link that she spun in circles with her fork. "I had a dream last night."

Brody leaned forward. "Do you want to tell me about it?"

"Yes, if you don't mind."

"I don't mind."

Memory spent the next few minutes telling Brody about her dream. The deputy didn't interrupt her or say anything until she was finished. He then waited for her to dry her eyes.

"So the little girl staring out the window was you?" he asked.

"Yes, I think so."

"And the man in your dream. You think he's your father?"

"Maybe," she answered.

"Who's the woman? Your mother?"

Memory turned her head upward. "Maybe… I don't know… What do you think?"

Brody didn't know what to say. He just stared at her. "I don't know. It could be a memory or just a dream… What about the rest of it?"

Her eyes filled with water again. "I don't know. I was scared, and I didn't know what to do. He was going to hurt me. I woke up, and the next thing I knew, I was in your bed… I'm sorry for invading your privacy like that."

The deputy stood and placed his hand gently on her shoulder. "You've been through a lot. It wasn't an invasion."

"Thank you." She placed her hand over his and leaned her head against his arm.

Brody knelt and took both her hands into his. He looked into her green eyes and smiled.

She smiled back. "You're my hero. Did you know that?"

He laughed and dropped his head down. She took her hand and ran it through his hair. He looked up at her. She smiled again, leaned in, and kissed him.

Brody didn't pull away, even though he knew he had just crossed the line.

⚜

The pain in Jeff's shoulder intensified when he turned the steering wheel of the Honda Civic to park in one of the pharmacy's parking spots. The hired gunman had found the coupe in the parking lot of the hiking trail, just as he'd thought he would. After a quick search of the vehicle, he found a flat-head screwdriver in the trunk and used it to punch the ignition. Hotwiring cars and punching ignition switches was a valuable skill he, along with most other military operators who'd worked in war-torn countries, had been taught.

The pharmacy looked busy, and before getting out of the Civic, Jeff tilted the rearview mirror downward and examined himself. *Damn, I'm a mess,* he thought as he licked his fingers and scrubbed the dirt smudges from his face. He used the hoodie he found in the back seat to cover his blood-stained T-shirt before going inside.

In the pharmacy, the hired gun made his way to the aisle where bandages and other wound supplies were kept. The killer soon found what he needed and headed for the registers. Jeff made sure the hoodie stayed over his head as he paid for his things. When he handed the clerk the money, he was surprised to see the woman in line next to him. Quickly, he dropped his head, collected his change, grabbed his bag of supplies, and hurried back out to the Honda. He opened the door, threw his bag into the passenger seat, and sat. He then eased himself farther down into the seat and waited for her to exit the building. After a few minutes, he saw the woman come out, toss a plastic bag into her Jeep's back seat, and climb in.

As the woman pulled out onto the highway, she didn't notice the red Honda Civic behind her. Jeff had recognized his former hostage in the pharmacy. After she'd pulled out of the parking lot, he followed her. The killer was out of options. He couldn't leave town yet, and he needed someone to help him with his wound. Jeff determined that he would follow the nurse to her place, kidnap her, and force her to take care of his shoulder—and anything else he needed—before he left town.

After getting the call from Deputy Katz, Harper drove to the pharmacy, selected the various makeup and hair products he had requested, and headed toward the sheriff's office. The nurse was excited to see her former patient. She was also eager to update Brody on Detective John Wilson's improved condition. The nurse taking care of the detective was a friend of Harper's, and she had called her early this morning with the good news. The sounds of rock and roll blared from the Wrangler's speakers as Harper cruised down the road with a desperate killer right behind her.

CHAPTER 8
NOTHING BUT MEMORIES

The drive down the hill from Brody's cabin to the main road was uncomfortably quiet. Neither the deputy nor Memory said anything about the kiss they had shared earlier. Brody's thoughts drifted between crossing the line of professionalism and taking advantage of an emotionally overburdened woman.

Memory's thoughts were consumed with regaining her memories and discovering who she was. *I think I'm a good person,* she told herself as she looked out the window at the Colorado pines. She then turned and looked at the man sitting next to her. He smiled when he caught her staring. *Why is someone trying to kill me? Am I a bad person?* she asked herself and then returned the smile.

"The sheriff wants us to stay here while you two are away," the deputy said after Brody stopped and rolled the window down.

Brody nodded in agreement. "Yeah, I think that's a good idea. We'll be back shortly. Make sure no one comes through."

"You got it," the deputy replied and stepped back toward his cruiser.

Brody pulled his Land Rover onto the highway and headed for the sheriff's office. He decided it was time to break the silence.

"What…"

"Do you think I'm a good person?" Memory blurted before he could finish his thought.

Brody was surprised by her question. He looked at her, back at the road, and at her again. "Are you talking about the kiss?"

She embarrassedly grinned and looked down at the floorboard. "No, I'm just wondering…"

"What?" he asked.

Memory lifted her head and stared into his eyes, unblinking. "People have tried to kill me twice now, and I don't know why. The only thing I can think of is that I've done something bad. Why would someone want to kill me—if I'm not a bad person?"

Brody watched as her eyes filled with water. He took her hand into his and pulled the Defender onto the side of the road. He then placed his hand gently under her chin, lifted her head, and wiped the tears from her cheeks. "Trust me. You're not a bad person. I'm a pretty good judge of fish—I mean people—and I'd know you're a good catch… person!" he said with a quick wink and playful grin.

Memory laughed aloud. She squeezed his hand, leaned in, and kissed him.

Brody reached his arm around her waist and pulled her closer. He kissed her deeply. If there was a line he was crossing, he didn't see it, nor did he care to see it. *This feels right,* he told himself.

Harper turned left into the sheriff's office parking lot just as Deputy Katz and his passenger were parking. The nurse pulled into the spot next to them and hurried to her patient.

"How are you feeling?" she asked while carefully pulling Memory's hair back to examine her head wound.

"I feel okay," Memory answered.

Harper smiled and gave the deputy a disapproving glare. "The wound needs to stay covered."

Brody raised his arms to his side and held his hands out. "I didn't have any bandages."

Memory placed her hand on the nurse's shoulder. "It's my fault. I took the dressings off," she said in Brody's defense.

Harper turned toward her patient. "Okay, I'll run up to the hospital, get some things, come back here, and redress the wound."

"Sounds like a plan. Now, if you don't mind, I'd like to take her inside," Brody said in a half-professional, half-joking tone.

Harper placed her hands on her hips. "Fine! I'll be right back!" she replied in the same tone.

Brody smiled. "Good, we'll wait inside."

Jeff Doyle sat in the Honda across the highway after following the nurse to the sheriff's office, where he was surprised to be seeing the woman he had been hired to kill. Many thoughts ran through his mind, but the one that kept coming up was the one where he walked away from it all with some cash in hand. He placed the car in drive, pulled the coupe behind the car wash, and parked. He took his new cell phone out and dialed the number from memory.

"It's me. You still want the woman?" he asked and waited for Porter to answer. He smiled when he heard his employer say yes. "Good, I know where she is. I'll call you when I'm ready to meet. Bring my money and add another two hundred and fifty thousand to it for earlier. Don't try anything stupid this time, or I'll kill you and anyone else with you, just like the guys I put down in the cabin," Jeff ordered and abruptly ended the call.

Porter was surprised by the call from his hired killer, but he was pleased at the same time. He hadn't seen or heard anything in town. Manuel and Lance hadn't found Doyle at his place either.

"Good news, I hope," Manuel said sarcastically as he sat at the table next to the senator's man.

Porter turned and furrowed his eyebrows at the sicario. He was growing more irritated the longer he was around the cartel assassin. He took a deep breath and slowly let it out. "It was. The man you failed to kill last night has a line on the woman."

Manuel chuckled. He thought it comical that he was being blamed for the failed hit. "Let me know when you're ready to go," he said. He then stood and turned to leave.

"I will. First, I gotta go back to Denver to see the senator," Porter replied.

"All right. We'll take care of her when you get back." Manuel headed for the living room. "I'm also going to kill this Jeff Doyle before we're done!" the sicario said before walking out of the room. He smirked at Lance, leaning against the wall just outside of the kitchen.

"I know," Porter said under his breath.

Lance followed Manuel with his eyes until he sat on the couch. He turned back toward Porter and stood before his partner, then glanced over his right shoulder to ensure Manuel wasn't paying them any attention. "What of that?" he asked quietly.

Porter peered over Lance's shoulder into the living room. "We need to be ready to take care of him after killing the girl and Doyle."

Lance nodded that he understood, turned, and walked out of the kitchen.

The sheriff's office was mostly empty, except for a few deputies working on some reports. Memory stayed close to Brody as he led her down the hall toward Sheriff Paul Kendrick's office. She had an uneasy feeling about being around people she didn't know. When the two got to the sheriff's office, they found his door open. Sheriff Kendrick was sitting behind his desk, and a woman was sitting in a chair across from him.

"Sheriff," Deputy Katz said as he stepped into the office.

Sheriff Kendrick stood and walked over. "Deputy Katz... Good morning, please come in," he said and gestured for them to come inside.

Brody and Memory stepped into the office. The sheriff closed the door behind them and walked to the woman he had been talking to before they'd arrived. "Deputy Katz, this is Doctor Carolyn Vail. She drove in from Denver, and she's an expert in the field of amnesia."

Brody leaned in and shook the doctor's hand. "Nice to meet you," he said.

The doctor smiled. "You as well, Deputy, and the young lady behind you, I assume she is the remarkable woman I've heard so much about?"

Memory's brows raised, and her lips turned upward. "Yes, but I don't know if I'm all that remarkable."

"Oh, I don't know about that," the doctor replied. "Why don't you have a seat on the couch? I'd like to talk to you for a few minutes, if that's all right." She gestured toward the sheriff's large leather sofa along the back wall.

"Okay," Memory said and then walked over and sat down.

Sheriff Kendrick looked at Deputy Katz, then darted his eyes toward the door. Brody knew what it meant. He started to leave, with the sheriff right behind him.

Memory stood and grabbed Brody. "You're not leaving, are you?"

"Deputy Katz can stay if you'd like," Doctor Vail offered. She could see the patient felt more at ease with the deputy around her.

Brody placed his left hand over hers. "Yeah, I'll stay."

Memory sat back down. Brody looked at Sheriff Kendrick for approval. The sheriff didn't quite know what was going on, but if the doctor approved, then so did he.

"I've gotta speak to one of my detectives. I'll be back in a bit," the sheriff said before walking out.

Doctor Vail pulled her chair closer to Memory and sat. "Memory, my specialty is helping people recover their memory."

Memory's eyes lit up. "How?"

"Well, I sit here, and you relax on the couch. Then when we're ready, we just talk."

"That will get my memory back?"

Doctor Vail leaned closer to the patient. "Memory, there's really no cure for amnesia. In many cases, it can return just as quickly as it left. A familiar smell, a familiar taste, a place, or even a comment from someone can trigger it. My specialty is therapy, where I teach you how to relax and concentrate."

Memory dropped her head. She had hoped for better news.

Brody saw the disappointment in her eyes. "Hey, why don't you try it."

Memory lifted her head back up and looked into his eyes. She felt at peace and, most of all, safe. "Okay, I'll give it a shot."

"Great. Now, Memory, why don't you lie back on the sofa. Close your eyes and just make yourself really comfortable," the doctor suggested.

Brody grabbed the other chair in front of the sheriff's desk and pulled it closer to the couch. Memory twisted her body, pulled her legs onto the couch, and laid herself back.

"Are you going to hypnotize me?" Memory asked.

"Your mind is a little cluttered right now. I'm going to try to help you rearrange things. Make it a little neater… if I can," the doctor explained in a calm tone.

Memory laughed uncomfortably. "Sounds like hypnosis. I just don't want you to have me running around like a chicken when you're done."

"Well, I'm not that kind of therapist. No chickens. I promise," Doctor Vail assured and then turned the lamp on that was next to the couch. "Deputy Katz, can you flip that switch by the door? I would like the room to be a little less bright, please?"

Brody got up, turned the room light off, and sat back down. "Anything else?"

"No… Now, Memory, I'm going to start talking to you, and I'd like for you to close your eyes and listen to the sound of my voice."

After Memory closed her eyes, Doctor Vail turned toward Brody and put her finger against her lips. He nodded, letting her know he understood he needed to be quiet. He then listened as the doctor softly spoke to her patient. Brody had attended a comedy show once where a hypnotist had performed on stage. The comedian or hypnotist asked for volunteers from the audience. Those who volunteered were soon following the commands of the comedian. It was hilarious, and to his recollection, one volunteer mooed like a cow. The doctor could call her treatment anything she wanted, but it was nothing more than hypnosis to Brody.

It wasn't long before Memory was relaxed, her eyes remained closed, and her breathing was steady. As she lay there, she could hear Doctor Vail's voice. When the doctor told her to imagine being in a safe place, Memory saw a little girl sitting on a blanket that was spread out over a bright-white sandy beach. The girl on the beach was the same girl Memory had dreamed about earlier, but she was much younger this time.

A short distance away from the girl, a woman danced around while wearing a blue dolphin float. The woman was beautiful, and she seemed to be trying to coax the little girl to follow her into the water. Memory watched as the girl stood and wrapped her arms around the man sitting next to her. Then without warning, Memory heard his voice. *"It's okay, baby. Go to your mommy."*

"Mommy!" Memory said aloud.

Doctor Vail and Brody looked at each other when they heard the patient, but they said nothing. Memory continued to describe what was happening on the beach. The doctor only asked questions that would help clarify things Memory was telling.

"Memory, what's your mommy doing?" Doctor Vail asked.

"My name's not Memory!" she responded in an angry tone.

The doctor scribbled in her notepad that she had on her lap. "I'm sorry, what would you like me to call you?"

Memory did not answer. She turned her head to the right and looked at the man sitting on the beach next to her. It was at that moment when she realized she was the little girl. The man sitting next to her was her father. Memory smiled, and she saw him saying something, but she couldn't hear what he was saying. Memory tried to listen to him, but the waves and the woman's laughter seemed to silence him.

Memory shook her head from side to side. "My mommy wants me to get in the water, but I don't want to. I want my daddy."

Doctor Vail once again wrote in her notepad. "It's okay. You don't have to get in the water. Now, let's go somewhere else."

"Okay, where?" Memory asked.

"Can you tell me what happened to you a few days ago?"

Memory's eyes fluttered but remained closed. "I don't know," she quickly answered.

"That's all right," Doctor Vail replied and thought about how she could keep her patient talking. She turned toward Deputy Katz and decided on what to do. "Can you tell me about Deputy Katz?"

Memory smiled. "He saved me," she said in a happier tone. Brody smiled.

"Can you tell me how he saved you? What happened?"

Within seconds, Memory found herself back in the South Platte River. "I'm floating down the river. I can hear the water and a car. It's so cold!" she said as she crossed her arms over her chest.

"What else?"

"I gotta get out of the water. There's a log! I grab it and pull myself onto the bank. I'm scared."

"You're okay. Now, tell me about Deputy Katz."

"He wants to know what happened to me. I can't speak."

Doctor Vail continued taking notes. Brody started to recall the events of that day.

"Now what's happening?" the doctor asked, hoping her patient would continue.

Memory squinted her closed eyes. "Brody is carrying me, but he fell. He wouldn't let me go even when he fell again. He's so strong, and he's helping me. I feel safe now."

Brody's eyes began to water. A lump formed in his throat.

"Good. Now, how did you get into the river?"

Memory shook her head no. "I don't want to go back there!"

"You're safe. No one can hurt you," the doctor said to assure her.

"I'm running through the snow. It's dark, and I don't know where I am. He's got a gun! He shot it! My arm hurts. I'm sliding down a hill, and I fall into the river. It's so cold."

"All right, let's go back even further to where you were before you found yourself in the woods."

Memory's breathing started to get faster and heavier. "I'm in a basement. He handcuffed me to a pipe. I can't get away. I keep hitting something against the pipe. I'm crying for help!"

"Can you see or hear anything?"

Memory started to squirm on the couch. "Steps. He's coming down the stairs… He's behind me!"

"It's okay. He can't hurt you. What's around you?"

"I smell smoke."

"Is there a fireplace?" Dr. Vail questioned.

Memory shook her head. "No, he smells like a pipe or smoking tobacco. He's reaching down! He's going to kill me!" she screamed.

Memory was in distress. The doctor realized she needed to end the session. "All right, I'm going to count backward from ten. You're back on the beach with your daddy. You feel safe. When I get to one, you'll open your eyes and find Deputy Katz sitting next to you," she explained as she counted backward to one.

When Memory opened her eyes, she found Brody sitting next to her. He reached over and took her hand. "How do you feel?"

"I feel okay," she answered and looked at the doctor. "How'd I do?"

"Fine. Now, do you remember what we talked about?"

Memory nodded. "I remember being on the beach with my father."

Brody interjected. "Does it help with your memory?"

Memory tightened her lips and thought about it. "No," she finally answered.

Brody turned toward Doctor Vail. "What do we do now?"

"We can do another session in a couple of days. In the meantime, I'll show you some relaxation techniques that you can use to help you fall asleep or take yourself back to the beach. Hopefully, that's the place that helps you the most," the doctor answered.

"I hope so. Not knowing who I am is starting to scare me. I'm afraid I'll learn that I'm not someone I like."

Doctor Vail closed her eyes and smiled. "Someone with amnesia doesn't experience a personality change. Many studies suggest that as we get older, our personalities change but not from amnesia. I'm ninety-nine percent sure that the polite and open woman in front of me is the same woman she was a few days ago, before she lost her memory."

Memory cried.

Chapter 9
Memories

When Harper returned with the medical supplies she needed, she cleaned and rebandaged her patient's head and arm. Brody sat quietly while the nurse jokingly berated him for not tending to the patient better than he had. Memory occasionally glanced over at the deputy, doing everything she could to not laugh. Sheriff Kendrick and Doctor Vail spoke outside, where the others could not hear them. After thirty minutes, the sheriff stuck his head in and asked Deputy Katz to join him in the hall.

"Yes, sir?" Brody asked after shutting the door behind him.

"How are things at your place?"

The deputy's eyes narrowed. He didn't know what the sheriff was asking… exactly. "Things are fine. She's sleeping in my room. She had a bad dream last night, but other than that, things are good."

"Your room?" The sheriff suspiciously asked.

Brody realized how it sounded. "She's staying in my bedroom, and I'm in a guest bedroom!"

"Thank you for clarifying. Now, how do you feel about keeping her there? I could keep her here, but your place is isolated, and if someone comes for her again, then…"

"We can see them coming up the road where the deputies are on guard," Brody offered.

"Yes. If you say no, then I completely understand and, well…"

Brody held his hands up and waved them back and forth. "No, my place is fine. What about the FBI and the fingerprints?"

"We've run her prints a few times, and now they keep coming back to someone different each time."

"Is the entire AFIS system down?"

"No, that's just it. Since hers, we've run numerous prints, but all those came back without any issues. The FBI has assured me that they'll have it figured out by tomorrow afternoon."

Brody didn't say anything while he thought about it for a moment.

Sheriff Kendrick could see the look on his face. "What is it?" he asked.

The deputy tilted his head toward his boss. "Did we get prints back on the guy at the hospital?"

"Yeah, he's a former police officer."

"Former police officer?" Brody asked, repeating the words.

Sheriff Kendrick nodded. "Yeah, what are you thinking?"

"One man held her somewhere, but two men showed up at the hospital to kill her."

"Yeah—just a minute. I gotta take this call," Kendrick said right before turning and walking away to answer his cell phone.

Brody thought about the two men at the hospital. *Were they hired guns?* he asked himself.

"Well, my day just got worse," Sheriff Kendrick said when he walked back toward Brody.

"Oh, yeah?"

"Yeah, there was a cabin fire on Rampart early this morning, and it looks like there are two bodies inside. The fire chief just called to let me know. Probably a couple who rented the place and didn't know to keep the fireplace screen closed."

Brody's eyes widened. "Where's this cabin?"

Sheriff Kendrick paused before answering. "Off Service Road Three Fifteen. Why?"

"I need a computer," Deputy Katz blurted and rushed to the first desk he saw. "What's the address?"

The sheriff pulled his notepad from his front pocket and flipped it to the cabin's address. Brody typed it into the computer and moved the white mouse arrow over the map.

"That's it," Sheriff Kendrick said when the map of the cabin, along with the Rampart Mountain Range, appeared on the screen. "What are you looking for, Katz?"

"This," he answered.

The sheriff leaned closer. "What?"

"The South Platte River. This is where I found Memory, and this is where the cabin is," Brody advised.

"How far away is that?" the sheriff asked.

"Just over a mile. If Memory was held in that cabin and ran toward the river when she escaped, then she had to fall off the mountainside and slide down into the South Platte somewhere over here," Brody explained as he moved the mouse around the screen, measuring the distance from one location to another.

"We need to identify those bodies and fast," Sheriff Kendrick said loudly as he took out his cell phone and headed for the exit. "Get her back to your place and wait until you hear from me."

Senator Livingston sat in his home office, browsing the internet for new beachfront properties in North Carolina. In a few months, he planned to be on the deck of his new beach house. He smiled and imagined himself reclining back in a comfortable patio lounger, sipping a mojito. At the same time, he enjoyed the view of the Atlantic Ocean as the sunset behind him.

What are you smiling about?" Frank Walters asked with a bitter tone as he entered the room. The drug smuggler had heard about Manuel's men being killed, and he didn't think there was anything to be smiling about.

"Nothing," the senator answered and closed the screen.

Frank took a seat on the leather sofa across from his bought politician, picked up his glass, and took a sip. He then glared at the statesman. "How much?"

Livingston was caught off guard by the question. He knew what Frank was asking, but he didn't know how to answer it. "How much? I don't understand."

Frank chuckled and took another drink. "You know exactly what I'm talking about. How much do you get once your wife dies?"

The soon-to-be widower turned and stared out the window. "Enough."

"Enough!" Frank got up to slowly walk to the senator and stand behind him. Frank was an intimidating man when he needed to be, and right now, he needed to be just that. "Vince, how much are you getting?"

The crooked politician was afraid. "Fifty million," he blurted.

Frank shook his head. "So I assume this entire fiasco with the girl has cost you nearly two and a half million dollars thus far? Am I correct?"

"No."

"No?" Frank circled the room. "I would have expected that it would've cost you the customary five percent for the kind of work you've needed to do. In your case, that would be two and a half million dollars, and if you haven't spent that much, then how much did you spend to take care of this girl?"

Livingston paused before answering. "Fifty thousand," he embarrassedly admitted.

Frank glared at the man. "You cheap son of a bitch!" he yelled.

"What's going on?" Porter asked after entering the room.

"Your boss just told me how much he spent to take care of this girl. I want to know why you decided to hire a fool like Jeff Doyle to do the job."

Porter had never told Frank the name of the man he had hired to kill the girl—just his address. Now, he knew that Manuel had spoken to Frank, which was something he needed to remember. "I thought he could take care of it, and the senator only put a fifty-thousand-dollar price tag on the job. There's not much that fifty thousand can buy for something like this," Porter explained and shifted his eyes toward his employer.

Livingston clenched his jaw and lowered his eyebrows, then stood. "Fine! I made a mistake. What you two need to do now is find a way to fix it!" he shouted.

Frank stepped toward the senator. "I will. You just get five million ready to be wired from your private account in the Cayman Islands."

"That's a lot of money to transfer overseas to an account in the United States. It'll get flagged," the senator snapped.

Frank laughed. "No, it's not coming to the States. It's going into my account in the Caymans. I'll arrange everything from here on out."

"What do you want me to do?" Porter asked.

"You go back and take care of your friend who screwed this whole thing up in the first place. Then you, Manuel, and the other men I'm sending to help will kill the girl and anyone else who gets in the way. This ends tonight! Do I make myself clear?"

"Yeah, I hear you, but Doyle wants seven hundred and fifty thousand tonight. He won't tell us where the girl is unless I have it when we meet with him," Porter said.

Frank nodded. "Anything else?"

Porter darted his gaze to Livingston and then back to Frank. "Yeah, my guy and I need five hundred thousand for this. Our lives are on the line," he answered. Porter was tired of working for the senator, and he decided it was the right time to walk away.

Frank walked toward Livingston and stood on the other side of the desk from him. "You see, this is what happens when you shop for deals. Right now, we're at over a million dollars, and that's all I've been told thus far. I'm sure it's more and—"

Livingston slammed his hand on the desk, interrupting the drug smuggler. "It is more, but it's still a long way away from five million," he barked and started to take a drink.

Frank slapped the drink from Livingston's hand right as the glass touched his lips. The glass shattered against the wall, and the senator fell back into his chair. He was afraid and looked to Porter for help, but his bodyguard just watched.

"Two other men are dead. These men have families in Mexico, and they will be compensated for their loss. That's another five hundred thousand for each dead sicario. Now, the rest of the five million is for paying these new men I have coming to take care of your problem. All of which will help you get your fifty million when your wife finally takes her last breath. You must spend money to make money," Frank explained and headed for the door.

"What about the money I need tonight?" Porter asked.

Frank turned toward the bodyguard and cleared his throat before speaking. "Follow me back to my place, and I'll get it for you," he ordered and left the office.

Porter gave the senator one last look before following Frank.

After a few minutes of thinking about what had unfolded, Livingston received a text. He picked up his phone and looked at the message. The senator huffed, dropped the phone on the desk, logged into his bank account in the Cayman Islands, and transferred the five million dollars to the account number Frank had texted him. The senator was upset, but there was nothing he could do except pay the price and hope things worked out. All the money the corrupt politician had in his Cayman account had come from his business dealings with Frank and his associates. The past eight years had been lucrative. Livingston had amassed ten million dollars, but now he was left with half of that, and he didn't like it.

The senator was still lamenting over the money he had just lost when his cell phone rang. He looked at the number and quickly answered the call.

"Yes, what is it?"

Brody wasted no time getting Memory in the Land Rover and heading back to his cabin. Harper insisted on staying with her patient to finish tending to her wounds. Now, the nurse was in her Jeep, following them up the dirt road to his mountain cabin. It wasn't the best option, but Harper wasn't taking no for an answer.

Since getting in the Defender, Brody hadn't said anything to Memory. She believed his thoughts were on something he wasn't sharing with her. After checking in with the two deputies at the entrance to his dirt road, Memory reached over and placed her hand on his.

"Something's bothering you. Did something I said earlier with Doctor Vail upset you?" she asked.

Brody glanced at her and then back at the road, twice. He didn't know what to tell her, but the truth seemed the right choice. "There was a cabin fire."

"Do you think it has something to do with me?"

Brody bit his lip before answering. "Yes. Well, maybe."

Memory felt he wasn't telling her everything. "Why do you think it involves me?"

Brody kept his eyes on the road avoiding the question. He didn't want to frighten her.

"Brody, please, why do you think it could be part of what happened to me?"

"They found two bodies in the cabin," he finally answered.

Memory nodded and looked at her reflection in the side mirror. "I guess it could just be a coincidence."

Brody thought for a moment before telling her the rest. "The cabin is less than a mile from where I found you in the river."

"Well, the cabin's location makes the theory that it's a coincidence less likely.," she replied.

Brody pulled into his driveway. "Yeah, it does. Let's get you inside and have Harper finish dressing your head wound."

Memory gave Brody a half smile. "Yeah, sounds good," she replied before opening the door and getting out.

Harper walked up to Brody after seeing Memory go into the cabin. She could tell something wasn't right. "What's wrong?"

Brody took a deep breath and blew it out. "She's a woman who doesn't know who she is, where she's from, or why someone wants to kill her."

Harper placed her hand on his shoulder. "Well, there's not much you or I can do except wait. I think she'll get her memory back, but it will take time," Harper said and walked toward the cabin.

Three firefighters searched what remained of the expensive cabin that had burned earlier. Two deputies stood sentry since the sheriff was notified about the two bodies found inside. As Sheriff Kendrick walked through the fire scene, he was accompanied by Fire Chief Robert Wilkins.

"What'd you think, Paul?" the chief asked.

Sheriff Kendrick turned to look at his old friend. "I don't know, Rob. What do you think happened?"

"Arson," he answered.

"You've already made that determination?"

Rob nodded, turned, and pointed at a spot on the floor. "One of the bodies was found there. It looks like he was covered in an accelerant and then lit on fire. The fire spread from him across the floor to his friend, who we found close to the front door. I think the accelerant was mostly used to cover the two men," the chief explained and then lit a cigarette.

Sheriff Kendrick gave the chief a curious expression. Something the man said piqued his interest. "How do you know they were men?"

"I was here when the coroner arrived and helped load them into the van. They weren't completely burned. Their faces and torsos were badly burned, but their lower portion was pretty much intact. Trust me… They were men."

"Oh," the sheriff replied and then looked around. "Does this cabin have a basement?"

"Yeah, it's over here, down these stairs. There used to be a door, and a set of stairs over them," the chief explained as he walked the sheriff to the stairs that led to the lower level.

Kendrick looked down at the debris-covered stairs. "Can I go down there?"

"Yeah. Most of the fire was confined to the main level and the second floor. There's smoke damage in the basement, but that's about it."

Sheriff Kendrick started down the stairs, careful not to trip over the still-glowing embers lying about. It was dark when he got to the bottom, so he took out his cell phone and turned on the flashlight app. He took his time examining anything that appeared out of the ordinary. When he got to the mechanical room, he saw something on the floor next to the water heater. His eyes widened, and he quickly moved closer.

"You've got to be kidding me," he said and photographed the object from different angles with his cell phone. The sheriff then bent to look at the handcuffs he found lying on the concrete floor. Sheriff Kendrick took his radio out and called for one of the deputies upstairs to bring him an evidence bag.

Senator Livingston stood at the foot of his wife's bed, watching as the nurse cleaned the saliva from Linsey's mouth. When the nurse was finished, she stood next to the senator. She motioned for him to follow her into the hallway.

"Sir, I've already called your wife's doctor and updated him on Mrs. Livingston's condition," she explained.

"Has there been some change from this morning?"

"Yes, your wife's vitals are dropping, and it seems she is approaching the end of life. You may want to prepare yourself. She may not make it through another night."

Livingston took a deep breath, held it in for a moment, and ran his hands across his face. "Thank you, I will. Just make sure she's comfortable, please. I don't want her to be in any pain," he pleaded as his voice cracked. If the senator was good at anything, it was acting. The only thing that concerned him about his wife's death was the young woman who was still alive. He excused himself and rushed back downstairs to his office. He shut the door, took out his cell phone, and called Porter.

"Yeah," the bodyguard said when he answered the senator's call.

"Look, I know you're upset with me, but you're the only one I can count on right now," Livingston confessed.

"What do you want?"

"I need to make sure the girl dies. You don't leave until you know she's dead. She must die before morning. Sooner would be better!"

"What do you think we're doing?" Porter asked in a frustrated tone.

"I know you are. Unfortunately, the men you're working with don't know the importance of timing limitations in all of this. I can't have them changing their mind and doing it tomorrow afternoon or night. It must be done tonight!" the desperate politician said and took a seat in front of his computer.

"Look—" Porter was about to protest when he heard a familiar chime. It was an alert from his banking app notifying him of some unusual activity. Like most people in his line of work, he kept his money overseas. He took his phone from his ear and opened his banking app. His forehead creased, and his eyes widened.

"Did you get it?" the senator asked.

"Yeah, five hundred thousand dollars," he answered.

"I'll triple it if you make sure it gets done tonight."

"Okay," Porter replied.

"By the way, I don't expect anyone to make it back here but you."

Chapter 10
Storms

The sun had dropped behind the mountains to the west, and a cool breeze blew through the valley, bringing in large dark-purple clouds. Brody stood on the deck in front of his stainless-steel grill, monitoring the steaks he had cooking. He drank a diet soda and stared at the bright-yellow-and-blue flames. He craved a beer, but that wasn't the right call tonight, primarily since he had not heard from the sheriff since leaving the office hours ago. Memory and Harper had spent most of the evening in his bedroom. The deputy didn't know what the women were doing, but a smile crossed his face when he heard them laughing.

Brody was placing the steaks on a plate when he heard someone walking up behind him. He turned around and found Harper standing there. She had a big grin across her face.

"What?" he asked.

"I'm pleased to introduce you to Ms. Memory," the nurse said. She waved her arms from side to side as if she were ushering someone along.

Brody smiled when Memory stepped out onto the deck. She was wearing black yoga pants, a black T-shirt, and flip-flops. Her blonde hair was straight yet circled around her face. Harper had helped her apply some makeup that drew attention to her eyes.

"Wow," Brody blurted.

Memory placed her hands under her chin and fluttered her eyelids. "You approve?"

"Yes. You look beautiful. Is all this the work of Harper?" he asked and looked over at the nurse.

"Actually, no! I just provided the makeup, shirt, yoga pants, and flip-flops. It was all her."

"How? I mean…"

"Muscle memory, I guess," Harper said as she shrugged her shoulders.

Memory leaned over and drew in the aroma of the grilled steaks that Brody held. "Smells good."

Brody pushed the plate closer to his houseguest and then slowly shifted it to in front of Harper. "I hope you ladies are okay with these steaks."

"Yes!" Harper happily replied.

Memory tilted her head to the right and lifted her shoulder to her chin. "Maybe! We'll know in a few minutes," she answered. She then pointed to her head and frowned. "Lost my memory recently."

Brody and Harper looked at each other. Neither knew what to say. They then turned back toward Memory, who had a large grin on her face. All three laughed aloud.

"C'mon, let's get inside," Brody suggested as the dark clouds above opened and began dropping heavy rain across the valley.

The coroner's office in Colorado Springs was closed. Sheriff Kendrick sat in his SUV, waiting in the parking lot for the deputy coroner to arrive. The sheriff needed to see the bodies from the fire, and the deputy coroner was the only person who could let him in on such short notice. Unfortunately, the deputy coroner was busy recovering another body in a small community outside the city. All Sheriff Kendrick could do now was wait. At about eight thirty, Kendrick saw the headlights of the coroner's van pulling into the parking lot. He got out and quickly approached the gate entrance.

"Rick, how's it going?" the sheriff asked when Deputy Coroner Rick Cooper rolled the driver's window down.

"Good, how's business in the mountains?"

"Well, the fire we had is pretty interesting," Sheriff Kendrick admitted.

"That's what Doctor Miner told me. He called and said I needed to hurry back here to meet you."

"Yeah, I need to see the bodies from the fire."

"All right. Jump in."

Sheriff Kendrick walked around to the passenger side and climbed in. "I've never been in the coroner's van," he remarked as he shut the door.

"Yeah, well, people are dying to ride in it."

Kendrick laughed. "That was bad."

"Well, the people I hang out with have never complained about my jokes. Right, Fred?" Rick shouted over his shoulder at the recently deceased man in the black bag in the back of the van.

The storm rolled in, pouring rain on the small, dilapidated mountain house outside Woodland Park. The front porch was missing some boards, one support beam was bent, and another was missing. The inside décor matched the outside with its outdated wallpaper, leaking pipes, and roof. To say it needed some TLC was an understatement, but it was the place Jeff Doyle called home.

Porter and the others arrived at Jeff's place after he'd texted them. They found the former SEAL sitting on his deck, wearing his tactical gear and his AR-15 at the ready. Porter parked the car and looked at Manuel in the passenger seat. The sicario's face was tight. He gripped the gun's pistol in his waistband as he glared at the man who had killed his friends.

"After the job is done," Porter said to remind him.

Manuel nodded and removed his hand from the gun. "Yes, amigo," he replied and got out.

Porter and Lance followed Manuel to the edge of the porch. Lance tossed the heavy money bag at Jeff's feet.

"Your money, as requested," Porter stated.

Jeff kept his eyes on the Hispanic man with the cartel tattoos, who seemed to be staring him down. "Thank you," he replied, his eyes locked on the man he believed was a sicario and who was responsible for the shoulder wound he had. "Is there a problem, compadre?" he sarcastically asked.

Manuel chuckled. "No. No problem. I hope you understand. It was just business earlier—compadre."

"Yeah, business," Jeff replied in agreement.

Porter was growing tired of the cat-and-mouse game. "Where's the girl?"

"No, that's not how it works. You'll follow me, and I'll let you know when we get there. Then we'll take care of the girl together," Jeff explained in no uncertain terms.

"How'd you find her?" Manuel asked.

"By luck. I saw her at the sheriff's office and followed her to a private road."

"Do you have a plan?" Lance asked.

"Yeah, I made a sand table on the side of the house. Come with me," Jeff ordered.

A sand table was a large and detailed layout of a target location. "All right," Porter said and followed his old friend. He was glad to hear that the former SEAL had a plan. Suddenly, everyone heard another vehicle coming up the driveway.

"Who's that?" Jeff asked as he took on a shooting stance with his AR-15 at his shoulder.

Manuel stepped in front of the SEAL. "Hold on, amigo.

They are my new soldiers."

Jeff glared at Porter. He didn't like surprises. "Fine! Try to keep them alive this time," he said sarcastically and started for his sand table once more.

Manuel turned toward Porter and smiled. "I know, after."

⁂

Sheriff Kendrick stood in the exam room of the coroner's office while Rick retrieved the bodies from the refrigeration lockers. He needed to know who the men were and why they had been burned in the fire.

"Here's the first one," Rick said as he pushed a cart into the room and flipped on the bright surgical lamp that hung from the ceiling. The pungent odor of burned flesh filled the room when he pulled the sheet back.

"Wow! That's bad," the sheriff admitted.

Rick pulled a plum from his lab coat pocket. "Yeah, burned bodies stink," he agreed and took a bite of the sweet fruit.

Sheriff Kendrick stared at the deputy coroner with a vacant expression on his face.

"What?" Rick asked.

"Nothing," he answered and began examining the body. "Why isn't he completely undressed?" The sheriff now understood how the fire chief was able to determine the victims of the fire were men. The man's body, though badly burned, still retained his genitalia.

"Doctor Miner hasn't looked at him yet. When he comes in, I'll help him search the body for anything unusual, undress what's left, take X-rays, and the doc will perform the autopsy," Rick explained and finished off the plum.

Sheriff Kendrick stepped closer after noticing the man's chest appeared awkward. "What's this?" He pushed his index finger against the deceased man's chest. "It's hard."

Rick put on some gloves and placed his hands on the body.

"I think it's a thin tactical vest," the deputy coroner answered.

Sheriff Kendrick gave Rick a blank look. "A tactical vest?"

"Yeah, I think it's a bulletproof vest."

Sheriff Kendrick put on a pair of rubber gloves and determined that it was indeed a bulletproof vest. He then looked at what remained of the dead man's hands. "What's this?" Kendrick asked and then pulled what was left of the shirt sleeve up.

"What do you see?" Rick asked as he leaned over to see what the sheriff was referring to. "Looks like a crappy tattoo."

The sheriff tilted his head and leaned closer to examine the ink. His eyes widened. "Damn it!"

"What is it?" Rick asked.

Sheriff Kendrick took his cell phone out and found the contact he was looking for. He immediately called the number.

"It's Sheriff Paul Kendrick. I need assistance," he told the man on the other end of the phone. "Yes, I know it's late, but this can't wait. I got one dead man who's a former cop, two dead sicarios, and a woman I can't identify because your agency's fingerprint database is broken," the sheriff explained to FBI Agent Dale Harper, the agent in charge of the Colorado Springs office.

Rain continued to fall, creating streams of water that snaked down the sides of the valley. Brody and his houseguests had finished dinner and were sitting in the living room, discussing the benefits of mountain living. The cabin builder happily shared his experience of building his own mountain retreat that he had always dreamed of. Memory and Harper enjoyed a glass of wine while listening to their host.

"I think I should be heading home," Harper announced as she stood.

Brody went to the sliding glass door that led to the deck. He looked up at the sky just as a flash of lightning streaked across it, illuminating the entire valley. He turned toward the other two. "I think you should—"

A loud clap of thunder shook the cabin.

Everyone jumped, and their eyes widened. Then in unison, they all laughed.

"As I was about to say, I think you should stay in the other guest bedroom. Getting through the valley will be like riding down a Slip 'N Slide. It's not something you should do in the dark in the middle of a storm."

"I agree," Memory said before Harper could object.

The nurse grinned. "I guess I'm staying then."

"Great! I think it's time for a good romcom," Memory said.

Harper quickly agreed. "Yes! That sounds like a good idea."

Brody rolled his eyes. Still, he gave in. "All right. See what you can find. I need to make a phone call." The deputy walked into the kitchen where he called Deputy Jackson, who was at the entrance of his private road from the main highway.

"Hey, Jack, it's Brody. Have you heard from the sheriff?"

"No, I haven't. Why? Was I supposed to?"

Brody had hoped there was some information about the bodies found in the cabin. "No, I was just wondering. How are things down there?"

Jackson laughed. "Wet. Have you not looked outside?"

"Yeah, I guess it is."

"Do you? I mean, we can change places if you'd like. I would love to be in a warm and dry mountain cabin with two beautiful women."

Now, Brody laughed. "Hey, it's not all fun and games up here either. I'm about to sit down for a romantic comedy."

"You can complain all you want, but Deputy Barnes and I are talking about his wife's horrible cooking in this truck. I'd trade with you in a heartbeat."

"I get it. I'll tell you what. In the morning, I'll bring you guys some eggs, bacon, and potatoes."

"You better! I'll talk to you later," Jackson said and ended the call.

Porter was sitting in the car parked on a dirt road along Highway 24 near the target's road. He and Lance were waiting for Jeff to call as planned. Porter wondered how long it would take Manuel and his three new men to make their way up the backside of the mountain to the target's cabin. He was still running the plan through his mind when he received a text.

"Damn," he said after reading the message.

Lance looked at his partner. "What?"

"The FBI is involved, and my guy can't keep the girl's fingerprints hidden anymore. He said they'll know who she is within the hour," Porter answered.

Lance nodded. "What do we do now?"

"We finish the job and get the hell out of town."

Jeff Doyle quietly made his way through the woods, making sure he stayed within the shadows of the dark pines. He slowly but steadily hiked upward toward the cabin with each minute that passed. At twenty minutes before ten, he got to his spot and got comfortable while waiting for the others to get into place.

Manuel followed the map and Jeff's directions as he led his men up to the target from the national forest. It took longer than expected due to the overweight, out-of-shape soldier who brought up the rear. "Rapido!" he whispered in an angry tone.

The other two sicarios, Marcos and Lupe, looked at each other and grinned. The overweight man was Carlos, and they knew he wouldn't move at any faster pace than he had already been.

Sheriff Kendrick was stuck at the coroner's office, waiting for one of the FBI's Colorado Springs office members to arrive. He was growing more and more impatient with every second that passed.

Finally, he heard someone knocking on the front doors. Rick rushed over and opened them.

A man in jeans and a button-up shirt held up his FBI credentials. "Where's Sheriff Kendrick?" Agent Dillon asked in an agitated tone. Agent Dillon didn't like being called out so late by his boss, Agent Dale Harper, who had ordered him to assist the sheriff.

"I'm right here," Sheriff Kendrick said.

"Here," the agent said as he handed over a folded sheet of paper.

Kendrick took the paper and unfolded it. "What's this?"

"Your Jane Doe. The computer glitch with AFIS is fixed."

"Who is she?" the sheriff asked.

Agent Dillon chuckled. "As far as we can tell, she's no one."

"No one?"

"Yes, no one. She's just some woman from Florida. I investigated her background myself when I got the prints back."

Sheriff Kendrick looked up and glared at the agent. "She's not just some woman from Florida! I got two dead sicarios and a dead man who used to be a cop—who, by the way, nearly killed one of my deputies and was most likely involved in the kidnapping of this woman!"

The agent shook his head. "Sheriff, if you have dead cartel sicarios in your jurisdiction, then that's a job for the DEA."

"What about the woman? She was kidnapped and raped, just in case you didn't know."

"I checked her out. She arrived in Denver a couple of days ago, and no one has reported her missing. Since she wasn't unwillingly taken across state lines, it still isn't a job for the FBI."

"That's crap!"

"Crap or not, that's the current situation," Agent Dillon said as he headed back to his car. "Call me if you get anything else that might fall under the FBI's jurisdiction. It's late, and this was a waste of my time."

"Hey, Agent Dillon," the sheriff called.

The arrogant agent turned and looked at the sheriff. "What?"

"If this turns into something bigger and you've ignored it, I'm going to punch you in the mouth," Kendrick stated.

"So now you're threatening a federal agent? You could get arrested for that," Dillon warned.

"It's a promise. As far as an arrest is concerned, who will make it?"

Dillon laughed at the elder law enforcement official. "You know what, Sheriff? If this turns into something the FBI has to look into, you have my permission to punch me in the mouth."

Kendrick watched as the agent sped out of the parking lot. He then turned toward Rick. "Thanks for the help," he said and hurried out to his car.

At midnight, Jeff heard Manuel's voice over the radio. "We're in place and ready."

Jeff keyed his mic. "We go in ten," he advised and then took out his last Fuente Fuente Opus X and lit it. He made sure to stay behind a rock, where the cigar's glow couldn't be seen by anyone inside. He took a long draw, held it in, and then slowly blew it out right before he flipped the switch on the small black box he held in his hand. "Can't have them making any calls," he whispered as he placed the cell phone jammer on the rock above his head. He then readied his AR-15 and looked up at the sky as another storm cloud rolled in.

"What's wrong?" Lance asked after seeing a concerned expression on his partner's face.

Porter turned. "I think this is going to get messy."

"What do you want to do?"

"There's nothing we can do except do what we're about to do. Now, wait five minutes, then pull up to the road. I'll come behind them. Do you remember what to do?" Porter asked.

"Yes, I'm to take the deputy who comes to my door, and you got the other one," Lance answered.

"Okay, let's do this!" Porter stepped out of the car and made his way into the woods.

Lance waited five minutes and pulled back out onto the highway.

⛰

Sheriff Kendrick drove through the mountain pass from Colorado Springs, heading back to Teller County. As he drove, the sheriff thought about the case and the woman. When he stopped at a traffic light in Woodland Park, he picked up the sheet of paper with her identity on it. *Why does someone want you dead?* he asked himself. The sheriff was still looking at the woman's photo when his cell phone rang.

"Sheriff Kendrick."

"Sheriff, it's Detective Warren. We got fingerprints from the handcuffs that you found in the burned-out cabin."

"Who is it?"

"A former Denver police officer named Jeffrey Eugene Doyle. He operates a private security company, and you're not going to believe this next part," Warren said.

"What?"

"The owner of the cabin that caught fire called. He said that Jeff Doyle takes care of the security cameras and checks in on the place for him," Warren explained.

"Where does he live?" the sheriff asked.

"Up here. I tried to call you earlier, but the storm seems to be causing some problems. I sent a couple of guys to his place, but he wasn't there."

"All right. Keep trying to locate Doyle and anything about him."

CHAPTER 11
DRIVE

The concrete was cold, and she was scared. She could hear an Irish song in between the clanging of the metal wrench that she was using to bang on the pipe. Her hands ached from the handcuffs that bound her to it.

"Please, help me!" she shouted over and over again. Suddenly, she heard a door open and then the unmistakable sound of someone walking down the stairs. "Please, help me," she pleaded once more.

"Why can't you just be quiet?" he shouted right before he hit her with something hard. Now her head was bleeding, and she was dizzy. The odor of his cigar lingered in the air, along with the disgusting smell of his alcohol-filled breath.

In an instant, she was no longer cuffed to the pipe. She was running through the woods with her kidnapper in pursuit. A shot rang out, and before she knew it, she was in the river, floating downstream. Her life was slowly coming to an end as she drifted in and out of consciousness. She thought of her father, William, and their time at the beach in Destin, Florida, where she grew up. "Daddy," she cried out.

William sat next to his daughter on the blanket. The sun was high in the sky, and William tried his best to get his daughter to go toward the woman. The little girl turned toward her father. "It's okay, you can go to your mommy," he said.

"Abigail, come to Mommy. C'mon, baby," the girl's mother begged.

A clap of thunder shook the cabin. Memory sat up in the bed, screaming. Brody and Harper rushed into her bedroom just as a bolt of lightning shot across the sky, followed by another clap of thunder. Brody flipped the lights on and stood by Memory's bedside.

"It's okay, Memory. We're here," Harper said reassuringly as she held her new friend in her arms.

Memory's breathing was labored. She was sweating, her body shook, and her eyelids blinked rapidly. "My… my… my…" She cried.

"What's wrong with her?" Brody frantically asked.

"It could be a seizure. Open the window. Her heart rate is racing!" the nurse shouted as she eased Memory back onto the bed.

Brody rushed to unlock the window and lifted it open. The curtains blew inward as a cool brisk wind carried by the storm rushed into the room. After a few minutes, Memory's breathing settled, and her heart rate leveled off. Harper ran a cool, damp cloth over Memory's clammy body.

Brody rushed back to his room and started to call 9-1-1 but quickly noticed that he had no service. Damn it," he whispered and headed back to Memory's room.

"She's okay," Harper said when the deputy walked in.

Brody saw that Memory was fully awake and aware. "Hey, pretty girl. You had me worried for a minute there." He sat beside her and put his arm around her shoulder.

"Memory, how do you feel? Can you tell us what happened?" Harper asked.

"I'm… I'm… I'm Abigail, but my friends call me Abby."

Brody and Harper had a look of bewilderment on their faces.

"Well, hello, Abby," Brody said with a smile.

"Yes, hello, Abby. May we call you Abby?" Harper asked.

The woman who had once been without identity remembered who she was. She also knew who her new friends were. "Yes, it's nice to meet both of you," she said and hugged them.

"Okay, I guess the most important question is what do you remember?"

Abby started to speak when another gust of wind blew through the window, carrying the scent of something Abby recognized. "That smell. It's him!" she cried.

"Who?" Harper asked.

"The man who hurt me. He's here!"

"Memory... I mean, Abby, it was just a dream coming from your lost memories. There's no one here but the three of us."

"No, I smell it too," Brody announced as lightning flashed and thunder roared. Without warning, the lights went out, leaving them in the dark.

"The storm knocked the power out," Harper said.

"Stay in here," Brody ordered and hurried out of the bedroom. He made his way to his room to secure his pistol and two additional magazines. Cautiously, he made his way to the sliding glass door. Slowly, he opened it, dropped down, and crawled out onto the deck. He carefully stood, pulled the cover from his telescope, and placed his eye to the eyepiece. Brody turned the scope in the direction of Deputy Jackson and Barnes.

He kept his eye on the same spot for a few minutes, hoping to see the familiar glow from one of Jackson's cigarettes. Unfortunately, there was no glow, just muzzle flashes followed by gunshots echoing through the valley.

Brody dropped down, crawled back into the cabin, and slid the sliding glass door closed. He kept his pistol at the ready as he maneuvered through his home, keeping close to the walls and in the shadows as he did. The deputy made his way back to his closet, grabbed a flashlight, closed the door, and tucked one of his shirts into the crack at the bottom. He turned the flashlight on and opened the safe he kept inside. He donned a tactical vest but then realized he only had it and one other bulletproof vest. The deputy thought about it for a moment and took it off. He fastened his drop holster to his thigh, grabbed his semi-automatic AR-15 shotgun, and turned the flashlight off.

Porter stood over the body of his partner. The deputy that had approached him got one shot off—one deadly shot. Porter stood there for a few minutes and glanced up at the mountain top at the cabin.

Jeff Doyle pressed his mic and spoke. "We must assume that the people inside heard those shots."

"We are still going in," Manuel ordered.

"Yeah, I know. I just wanted to let you and your men know. We don't want you to lose more men," Jeff commented sarcastically.

"No, amigo, we don't. We'll see you inside," Manuel replied and motioned for his men to execute the raid.

Brody entered the bedroom and quickly placed the bulletproof vests over Abby and Harper.

"I thought I heard gunshots," Harper nervously whispered.

"You did," he replied.

"What are we going to do?" Abby asked.

Brody took a breath. "Men are going to come in here. They are going to try to kill us."

"What are we going to do?" Abby asked again.

"You two are going to stay here for now. Abby, you take this pistol, and if anyone sticks their head through this window, you shoot it!" Brody instructed.

"Okay," she said with her voice trembling.

"What do you want me to do?" Harper asked.

"This is a semiautomatic shotgun. It has nine rounds in the magazine and one in the chamber. When you pull the trigger, one round will fire, and you don't have to be precise with it. Just keep an eye on the door, and if anyone walks through it or past it, pull the trigger and keep pulling it until they fall."

"I can do that," she replied.

"Good! Now, when you hear me yell 'Defender,' I want the two of you to climb out the window, run to my Rover—the keys are in it—and head right down the mountain. It will be slippery. Just point it downhill and go. When you get to the bottom, be ready for more shooters. Don't stop. Just stay on the gas and run for the sheriff's office," Brody ordered and started to leave.

Abby reached out and grabbed him by the arm. "What are you going to do?"

Brody could see she was worried. He gently placed his hand behind her head and pulled her against himself. "I'm going to make sure you get out of here. There's this girl I just met, and I'd like to get to know her a little better," Brody answered and kissed her softly.

"Brody, be careful. There's so much I want to tell you."

"I will. Remember 'Defender,' then run and don't look back. I'll see you later," he said and left the two of them in the room.

By the time Sheriff Kendrick reached Woodland Park, he hadn't heard from his deputy about Doyle. He took out his cell phone and called dispatch.

"It's Sheriff Kendrick. Have you heard from Deputy Warren?"

Sherri, the dispatcher, answered his call. "No, Sheriff. He and two other deputies are checking on some of the other mountain properties that Jeff Doyle manages security for. They could be out of radio and cell phone range."

The sheriff knew the mountains of Colorado were beautiful to look at, but they were horrible when it came to radio and cell phone communications. "What about Jackson and Barnes?" he asked.

"No, Jackson and Barnes are not due to check in for twenty more minutes."

The sheriff thought about it for a moment. "Sherri, call them and ask how things are going."

"You got it, Sheriff."

The cabin was dark and quiet. Rain steadily fell outside, creating an almost rhythmic sound on the metal roof. Brody kept his AR-15 at the ready as he stealthily made his way to a position that gave him a tactical advantage. He knew that whoever was coming for them would come up from the basement, the side windows, or the front door. *Maybe from all three entry points,* he thought as he knelt and kept an eye on the front door.

Carlos quietly approached the front door while Lupe laid himself prone just outside of it and readied his AK-47. Carlos looked at Lupe, who gave him the nod. In one slow but powerful movement, Carlos kicked the door open and ducked to the left, while Lupe directed rapid-fire shots through the cabin's front door.

Brody saw the muzzle flashes from the AK-47. He returned suppressive fire in the direction of the muzzle flashes of the assault rifle.

Lupe rolled out of the line of fire to his left but not before taking one round to his shoulder. He winced in pain and kept moving until he was out of the field of fire.

Carlos was the least experienced soldier. He stepped in front of the door and was met with a bullet to the head. The big man dropped to the ground and never got back up.

Jeff came into the cabin through the door under the deck. He cautiously made his way toward the stairs, and when he heard the shooting, he started up them.

Brody knew he needed to get the girls out and soon. He reloaded his rifle and stepped toward the front door when he saw the shadow of someone coming up the stairs from the basement. He quickly turned, but he wasn't fast enough. The shooter from the basement fired his AR-15 at Brody. Two bullets ripped through him, his left shoulder and thigh. Brody returned fire and forced the shooter to retreat to the basement.

Now, there was only one thing left to do. Brody ran out the front door and was greeted by a hail of gunfire. The deputy returned fire and took up position behind one of Harper's front tires. He reloaded and peeked through the wheel well and saw a man taking cover behind a mound of dirt. Brody carefully took aim at the man and fired his AR, dropping him.

Marcos watched Lupe go down before making his way to the woods near the side of the house. The woman, who he believed was still inside the cabin, was the primary target, not the man.

Brody took a moment to survey his surroundings and catch his breath. His pain was excruciating, but he had to ignore it. He turned toward his Defender and decided it was time. "Defender!" he shouted.

Harper and Abby heard the command. "Let's go!" Harper yelled. She took Abby by the arm and pulled her along. Harper pushed the window screen away, climbed out, and waited for Abby.

Abby placed one leg through the window but was grabbed by the hair and pulled back inside.

"Where are you going?" Jeff yelled as he threw her to the floor.

Abby recognized the man's voice, and she smelled the same cigar odor. Standing over her was the man who had kidnapped, raped, and attempted to kill her twice. She froze in place and watched as her tormentor raised his gun.

"No!" she screamed and aimed the gun Brody had given her at the man. She pulled the trigger repeatedly until the gun wouldn't shoot anymore.

Jeff dropped to his knees and fell forward onto Abby. She screamed and pushed him off. She got to her feet and stared at his lifeless body.

Marcos saw a woman standing next to a window on the side of the house. "The woman," he whispered as he raised the MP-5 and fired.

"Let's go!" Harper yelled from the window right before a bullet hit her in the back of her shoulder. She screamed and fell against the cabin.

Brody saw the shooter coming toward the house from the

wood line. He emptied his AR into the man but not before the attacker shot Harper a second time. "No!" he shouted and rushed to her, just as Abby climbed out of the window.

"Harper!" Abby screamed as she tried to lift her friend from the ground.

When Brody got to them, he dropped his AR and examined the nurse. "She's okay. The vest stopped the second bullet! But she needs to get to the hospital for her shoulder wound. C'mon!" he yelled as he dragged Harper toward the Defender. Abby reached down and helped. The two of them lifted the wounded nurse into the vehicle.

"You drive!" Brody ordered.

Abby ran around the vehicle and got in. She found the keys and turned the ignition. It started right up. Brody smiled at her and began to get in, but gunfire erupted from the corner of the cabin. Brody winced when another bullet entered his chest. "Drive!" he shouted and shut the door.

Abby stared out the window at the man who had saved her so many times.

"Drive!" he shouted once more as he pulled his 9mm from his drop holster and shot at the corner of his house.

Abby reluctantly hit the gas and sped away from the cabin. Tears streamed down her face as she steered the Defender down the slippery mountainside. The Defender bounced along over the road, splashing through one mudhole after another. The rain continued to fall, and the lightning raced across the night sky. Abby could still hear gunfire coming from the cabin as she approached the main road. Suddenly, someone stepped onto the road with his gun aimed at her. Her eyes widened.

Porter Rollins was about to end it when he felt a bullet enter his shoulder, forcing him to drop his gun. He grabbed the wound and looked to his right, at the man coming up from the highway.

"Don't move!" Sheriff Kendrick ordered as he approached the man.

Abby slammed on the brakes, skidding to stop. She jumped

out of the Rover, ran to the passenger side, and opened the door. "Brody is still up there! He's been shot, and so has Harper. They need an ambulance!"

The sheriff pushed Porter to the ground and handcuffed him. "Who are you?"

"I want my lawyer," Porter answered.

"You'll need one," the sheriff said and pressed the mic on his radio. "I need additional units to my location for an officer down and possible multiple casualties."

Gunfire echoed through the valley. Abby looked at the sheriff. "We're not getting back up that road any time soon," he said.

Brody continued to exchange gunfire with the shooter, who stayed in the shadows. He took cover on the opposite side of the cabin and checked his 9mm. The deputy had one round left, but then he saw the shotgun he had given Harper lying on the ground near the window. He limped over and picked it up. Slowly he made his way to the man who had shot Harper.

Manuel tried calling his men over the radio, but no one answered. He was alone, and there was still one target that needed to go down. Staying close to the side of the cabin, he cautiously made his way to its back. When he reached the corner, he peeked around the faux stone and searched the area under the deck. It was too dark to see anything. He took a breath and walked under the deck, keeping his weapon out in front of him. Under one of the support beams, he saw something. He aimed his rifle and inched his way toward it. As he got closer, he realized it was the figure of a man leaning up against the beam.

Manuel stepped out of the shadows and aimed his gun at the man's chest when he got close. "Now, you die!" he boasted and fired three rounds into the man's chest. "What?" Manuel whispered when he saw he had just shot Marcos's lifeless body. Quickly, Manuel spun around and found himself face-to-face with Deputy Brody Katz. The cartel's killer didn't have a chance. Brody put three rounds into the man before he hit the ground.

Slowly, the deputy limped forward and looked down at the

dead man for a minute, before turning and facing the highway, where he saw red and blue flashing lights. He dropped to the ground, leaned against his cabin, and watched the lights in the distance. He took a breath and closed his eyes.

CHAPTER 12
A NEW DAY

As the night turned to day, emergency vehicles lined the highway near the road leading to Brody's cabin. News media helicopters circled the sky, broadcasting the mayhem across the country. Abby sat in an interview room at the sheriff's office, waiting for news about Brody and Harper. The kind and caring nurse who had cleaned her wounds, fixed her hair, brought her clothes, and most importantly, took her in as a friend when she needed one the most was now in surgery. There was no news of Brody, whom she had last seen on the mountain.

"They're flying him to Colorado Springs," Sheriff Kendrick announced when he walked in.

Abby turned and rushed to the sheriff. "Is he going to be okay?"

"I don't know. When they found him, he was unconscious. I'm not going to sugarcoat it. From what they've told me, he's in bad shape."

The corners of Abby's mouth turned downward into a frown, and her eyes filled with tears. "He saved me. He's gotta be all right!" she cried and placed her hands to her face.

Sheriff Kendrick was never good at consoling victims. Still, he moved closer and placed his arms around her. "I'll get you down there just as soon as possible," he said.

"Sheriff Kendrick," a man's voice called from the doorway.

The sheriff turned and found Agent Dillon of the FBI standing there. "Just a minute," he said and turned toward Abby. "Why don't you go to my office for now? Try to get some sleep, and I'll come by shortly. Hopefully that'll give me time to get some information about our friends."

"All right," Abby replied and headed out of the room.

"I'll need to speak to you," Agent Dillon said as Abby passed in front of him.

Sheriff Kendrick stood in the agent's face. "She needs to rest. Besides, you and I have something to discuss in private."

Agent Dillon gave the sheriff a curious expression. "We do?"

Sheriff Kendrick shut the door behind Abby and turned toward the agent. "Yeah, we do. It has something to do with a promise I made."

"Sheriff, do you really think I will stand here and let you—"

Senator Livingston was sitting in his office, watching the news concerning the incident in the mountains. He was nervous and didn't know what to do. He hadn't heard from Porter or Frank. His wife lay in unconsciousness while her life continued to fade away. "Damn," he blurted when he heard someone knocking on the front door. The senator rushed over and opened it. "Frank! Have you heard anything?"

Frank, who was accompanied by another man, quickly stepped inside. "No, I can't get a hold of anyone." He tilted his head toward his associate and said, "Check the house."

The large man accompanying the drug smuggler made a direct line for the senator's home office with an electronic device of sorts in his hand.

"What's he doing?" Livingston asked.

Frank placed his finger against his lips, then mouthed, *Wiretaps.*

The senator's eyes widened. He turned his attention back to the man searching his office.

"We're clean," the bodyguard announced as he closed the top drawer of the senator's desk.

"Let's talk in your office," Frank suggested and hurried into the room before Livingston had a chance to object.

Livingston sat behind his desk while Frank's man acted as though he were checking the bookshelf behind the senator's chair for more wiretaps. The senator turned and looked at the man and then back at Frank.

"It's all clean," the man announced.

Frank nodded. "Good."

The senator held his hands open on the desk. "Frank, what in the hell is going on?"

"We need to tie up some loose ends."

The senator shook his head. "Loose ends? I agree. Where do we start?"

"Right here," Frank answered and pointed at his man. Before Senator Vince Livingston knew what was happening, he felt the cold steel of the barrel against the side of his temple. The corrupt politician never heard the shot that ended his life.

"Set it up and be quick about it!" Frank ordered. After seeing the mess on the news with Porter and their men, the drug smuggler had decided Vince was a loose end, and what was left of the five million he'd been wired was payment toward securing new business routes.

Frank's hitman took the gun he had found in the senator's desk when he'd first entered the office and put it into Livingston's hand. He then pulled a spray bottle from his pocket and covered the senator's hand with a mixture of barium, antimony, and lead—or gunshot residue, as it was more commonly known. The man then pulled the slide back and jammed the spent casing into it.

"Why are you doing that?" Frank asked.

"It's a malfunction with semiautomatic handguns when the

spent shell case fails to eject as it should. It's called a stovepipe and is something investigators look for in suicides with semiautomatics," the killer explained and then dropped the gun to the floor next to the senator.

"Good idea," Frank replied.

The killer looked at his employer. "Anything else?"

"No, let's get out of here," he answered and then rushed out with his hired man right behind him.

The nurse and one of the housemaids upstairs stood next to Linsey Livingston's bed. "What was that?" the maid asked the nurse after hearing a loud noise from somewhere in the house.

"I don't know. Go find out. I'll stay with her," the nurse ordered.

The maid walked out of the room and left the nurse with her patient.

Linsey Livingston opened her eyes, and with all the strength she had left, she pointed at her nightstand. The nurse already knew what she wanted, so she walked over and picked up the five-by-seven frame and handed it to Linsey, just as she had done many times before. The nurse always liked seeing the joy in her patient's eyes when she held the old photo of the little girl and herself on a beach many years ago.

The responding emergency medical crew pronounced Senator Vince Livingston dead at seven-thirty in the morning. Mrs. Linsey Livingston followed her husband in death at five o'clock in the afternoon on the same day. She was still holding the framed photo of her and her daughter, Abigail, when she passed.

One Week Later

The day started out beautiful, with blue skies overhead and the sun shining brightly. Abigail "Abby" Johnson had the top down of Harper's Wrangler as she drove to the hospital in Colorado

Springs. After parking the Jeep in the parking garage, she made her way to the entrance and took the elevator to the fifth floor. She was surprised to find Sheriff Kendrick and two other men in suits waiting for her.

"Paul, what's going on?" she asked, but then she had a scary thought. "Oh my, is… Did…" She placed her hand over her mouth.

Sheriff Kendrick immediately knew that Abby was thinking the worst. "No, everything's fine!" he quickly reassured. "These men are attorneys, and they need to speak to you."

"Hello, I'm David Stern with the law firm of Stern, Hamlet, and Briggs," the older of the two lawyers stated and reached his hand out.

Abby shook the man's hand and then looked at the other man.

"And I'm Bill Carnes," the other lawyer said as he reached out and shook Abby's hand.

"It's nice to meet you guys, I think. I don't mean to be rude, but why are you here to see me?" she asked.

"Well, there's a private conference room down the hall. The hospital administrator has agreed to allow us to use it. If you don't mind?"

Abby glared at the two men and then looked at the sheriff. "Okay, but he's coming too," she replied in a tone that told the lawyers it was non-negotiable.

Stern nodded. "Absolutely, that's perfectly fine."

Abby and the sheriff followed the two legal eagles into the private conference room and sat across from them.

"Ms. Johnson, you grew up in Destin, Florida. And your father—"

Abby shook her head. "My father passed away last year. I thought his estate was already settled. I signed a bunch of papers then."

The attorneys looked at each other and then back at Abby. "We're not here regarding the passing of your father. We're here regarding the passing of your mother."

Abby was confused. "I don't understand. My mother left us when I was five. I never saw her again, and from the time I was born until I was five, I only saw her like… maybe… five times."

David Stern looked out the window, then turned back toward Abby. There was only one thing to do: put it all out on the table. "I know. I've been your mother's… and her family's attorney for a very long time."

"My mother… Well, my mother disappeared and never came back. She never even bothered to reach out to me or cared one thing about what happened to me or—"

"That's not entirely true! Linsey cared very much for you and—" Stern stopped himself before saying anything else.

Abby was surprised by the attorney's interruption. "I take it you knew her pretty well."

"I did. I took care of every legal aspect of her life. She and my wife were very close."

Abby thought for a second. "Tell me about her."

David Stern opened his briefcase. "I think it'll be easier if I show you these while I tell you about Linsey Beaumont-Livingston," he said as he handed a stack of photos to her.

"Beaumont? I went to college on a Beaumont Scholarship," she said as she took the photos and flipped through them.

"Yes, I know. I set it up for you," David said while Abby looked through the photos.

"These photos… All of them are of me."

"Yes, your mother couldn't be in your life for reasons that could fill five legal pads. But she always knew what you were doing, where you were, and who you were with. She made sure that you never longed for anything," he explained.

"There're so many photos. How?"

David took a deep breath. "She hired a team of private investigators, bodyguards, and anyone else she felt you needed."

"I don't understand…"

"The business—"

Bill placed his hand on his colleague's shoulder and shook his head no.

Stern looked at his associate and then back at Abby. He was telling everything. It was time for secrets to be exposed. He politely pulled his arm away and leaned closer to Abby. "The business of your mother's family had put them at risk by many people and organizations worldwide. Your grandfather didn't care for your father. He did everything he could to keep your mother and father apart, but everything he did failed. Finally, your mother and father ran away, and that's when they had you."

"Why did she leave?"

"Your grandfather's men found your mother and brought her back to Colorado. He told her he would kill your father if she tried to return. She never told her father about you, and when he died, she took over the family business. Your mother wanted to reach out to you, but some of the family's enemies tried to kill her right after your grandfather's death. It was then she decided that she would never put you in a situation like that. She believed you were safer with your father than with her."

Abby turned toward Sheriff Kendrick. "I thought she didn't care about me," she confessed and then looked back down at a photo of her college graduation day.

"Sometimes, we never know why people do what they do, and unfortunately, we assume the worst," Sheriff Kendrick offered.

Abby lifted her head. "Well, thank you for the information, but I need to go see—"

David held his hand up. "Please, wait, there's more."

"What is it?" she asked.

"Your mother was forced into marrying a man" ," David said.

"Is he alive?"

"Senator Vince Livingston passed before your mother," Bill answered.

Abby interrupted. "I'm sorry to hear that."

David shook his head. "Yeah… Well, hold your condolences for now. There's more."

David Stern spent two hours informing Abby about her stepfather's bodyguard's confession regarding the senator's attempts to keep her mother's estate to himself—an estate that Abby learned was worth fifty million dollars, all of which would have gone to her stepfather in the event of her death.

When they were finished, Abby had a new attorney, a fortune, and pieces of a memory of her mother. David Stern promised to tell her more about Linsey when Abby came to Denver next week to sign papers. For now, there was a patient down the hall she desperately wanted to see.

EPILOGUE
MEMORIES TO LAST
A LIFETIME

The South Platte River was running high. Fishermen lined the banks while others waded through the strong current, busy casting their lines into the deep pools and hoping for a strike. The sun sat high in the sky, and the events from over a year ago were still discussed around the small mountain community. In the months that followed, Abby learned a lot about her mother's family, the kind of person Linsey Beaumont was, and the incredible nonprofits she had created to help those in need. All of it Abby was overseeing since being named as the sole beneficiary to the Beaumont estate.

As Abby sat at a picnic table enjoying a cold beer with Harper, she reflected on the events of the past year and the friends she had gained. The friends she had before being kidnapped were the same friends she had come to meet in Colorado for a weeklong hiking trip over a year ago. She'd enjoyed introducing her old friends to her new ones.

"Do you girls need another one?" Paul Kendrick asked as he dug through the cooler.

"No, I think we're good for now," Harper answered.

Harper used her hand to block the sun and looked out to the river where her fiancé, and newly sworn-in sheriff, John Wilson, stood next to his best friend, casting his line into a dark hole. "Catch anything yet?" she asked.

John turned toward the bank. "No, but he is."

Brody reeled his line in with a large trout on its end. He turned toward the bank and held the fish up for the others to see, with a big smile on his face.

"Don't brag! No one likes a bragger," John insisted.

"Jealous much?"

"No, not at all," John answered and glanced back at the others to make sure no one was close by. "Hey, did you get it?" he asked after turning back to Brody.

"Yeah," Brody answered.

"Well, let me see it."

Brody looked over his shoulder, dug into his pocket, and pulled out a small black box. "I'm worried," he confessed as he showed his friend the diamond ring.

"It's great! What are you worried about?" John asked.

Brody bit his lip. "She's a… and I'm a…"

"A man she's in love with. That's who you are."

Brody smiled. "Yeah, well, here it goes," he said and made his way to the bank.

He took off his waders, walked to the picnic table, and stood in front of Abby.

"Giving up so soon?" she asked.

The others stood and walked toward John, who had followed Brody out of the water.

Abby was surprised by their quick departure. "What's going on?"

Brody took Abby's hand into his, dropped to a knee, and smiled. He cleared his throat. "Abby, will you—"

"Yes, yes, and yes! A million times yes!" she shouted and threw her arms around his neck.

Brody held the catch of his life in his arms. He couldn't be happier. Abby had tears of joy running down her face. It was a memory to last a lifetime.

Also by Michael Merson

Heartbeats of a Killer

The Secrets of Taylor Creek

Roses in the Sand

Jaxson Locke Boxset Books 1-3

Double Down

Longshot

No Justice

Revenge

Beach Escape

COMING SOON

Key Getaway

ABOUT THE AUTHOR

Michael grew up in Pensacola, Florida, where he spent the summer months as a youth at the beach, tubing down the river or splashing around in a pool near his grandmother's home. After graduating from high school, he joined the US Army and served in the Military Police Corps. After nearly seven and a half years, Michael left the military. He took a position at the Colorado Springs Police Department, where he served the community for ten years. An injury on duty forced him into early retirement from policing. Currently, Michael is the Department Chair of the Criminal Justice Department at a local community college. Michael earned a Bachelor of Science in Sociology with an emphasis in Criminology from Colorado State University and a Master of Criminal Justice from the University of Colorado.

Michael started his writing career as a ghostwriter for a publisher of textbooks. Eventually, he co-authored a textbook. Michael has always had the desire to write fiction. Through the encouragement of his family and friends, Michael started writing mystery fiction and hasn't stopped. Michael's wife, Stefanie, still catches him daydreaming as he drives down the highway thinking about different stories. The facial expressions that he makes reveal to her that somewhere in his mind, he's reviewing a chapter, scene, or dialogue between characters for a new book.

Made in the USA
Monee, IL
04 January 2023

23952046R00085